In the Dark

The Cities Below, Volume 1

Jen Colly

Published by Jen Colly, 2025.

IN THE DARK

First edition. February 8, 2025.

ISBN: 979-8230663072

Written by Jen Colly.

To my husband Ryan, for all that you are, and all that you do. I love you.

To Sofia and Roger...you're too little to read this. Close the book. Love, Mom.

Thank you to the beautiful ladies of the DHA for steering me down this road, and to Renee and Mary for giving me the keys and teaching me how to drive.

Chapter 1

PARIS, FRANCE

The night was dark, the steady rain mottling the persistent light of the streetlamps. Darkness was a good thing. He wasn't comfortable here. This wasn't home, and a part of him hated Paris. For all the city's beauty and sophistication, it was a very dangerous place.

Stepping over a deep puddle, Soren moved as quickly as he could, keeping to the shadows as he scanned the quiet street, straining to hear any movement beyond the rain.

Though he usually didn't watch his back, or worry about what waited around the next corner, here in this city it made the difference between getting what he needed to survive, and the eradication of his people. If humans were to discover him, their fear would take over, and every last one of his kind would be hunted down and butchered. It had happened before.

Men's voices broke through the peaceful silence of night, and he ignored them, just as he ignored the rain dripping from his hair and off the tip of his nose. They were too far away to cause him any trouble. He was here for another, more urgent purpose. He'd ignored the signs, and now his body required sustenance.

Then a woman's whimpering plea fell into the mix of voices.

He changed his path, searching for her, and found her in a dead end alleyway. Two men pinned the helpless and frightened woman to the brick wall. He pulled the men from her, threw them hard against the

1

building. Their heads hit the bricks with a sickening thud, and the men fell to the ground, limp, lifeless.

The woman had been pitched back against the far building, taking a bump to her head. He spun around to see how she had fared. She still stood.

Hunger hit him hard.

He strode toward her, chest heaving from excitement, anticipation. The woman before him was water to a man dying of thirst.

She was so refreshingly ordinary, from her wet and clinging black hair, to her flushed cheeks. Even the cut of her shirt, low enough to show a mere hint of her bosom and all of her lovely neck, was simple.

She leaned against the building for support as she tested the back of her head for any serious injury. "Thank you. I don't know what I would have done."

Her trembling voice set him in motion, but her tentative smile sealed her fate. He moved a step closer, then another, crowding her.

She stumbled as she tried to step back, looking for an escape. The wall of the building was already pressing against her back. Still he advanced.

Standing inches from her, he grazed her cheek with his fingers then plunged them into her hair and swept the sopping mess back. She gasped softly, a nervous intake of breath.

"Please, don't." Her voice wavered.

"Say it again," he demanded roughly, though his touch was gentle.

"Please," she whispered, squeezing her eyes shut, and he dropped his head and nuzzled her neck. Her voice enthralled him so, had drawn him closer.

She whimpered, the vibrations touching his lips, and he tightened his grasp on her, trying to somehow remain focused. He needed to go slowly, but it had been too long. The sensation of her lush form against him was too right, the soft scent of her flesh too potent.

Control fled, and he bit her. Her body jerked once, then went rigid against him. Happily drowning in the sweet and tempting scent that had driven him over the edge, he barely noticed. Rose? Lavender? He didn't know flowers, and he didn't care to learn them, but he would never again breathe that scent without thinking of her.

Nourishing, sweet and hot, her lifeblood sent blissful shivers coursing through his body. Feeding was always a delicious experience, though he'd never experienced anything like this.

The rain continued to fall on them, the cool drops sliding down her neck to the very spot they were joined. Soren drank in the water, the taste of her skin infused into every raindrop. So intoxicating, so sensual. He couldn't help but wrap his other arm around her waist and bring her closer. He was no longer holding her still, but simply holding her.

His heartbeat raced. The simple act enough to send him out of his mind with satisfaction, but the soul wrenching pleasure of her clutching his shoulders had him gasping for breath.

The world faded away. No rain or alley, no feeding existed. He only wanted to bask in the way her fingers moved, tightening then releasing, like she needed him. Wanted him. But too soon her fingers slipped from his shirt, fell slowly down his arms, and hung at her sides.

She went limp in his arms. Something was wrong. Sealing the bite on her neck with a kiss of thanks, he pulled back. She'd passed out.

That wasn't supposed to happen. Losing consciousness occurred after a person had been either wounded or frightened. Any injury she had wasn't serious. If he'd frightened her, that posed a far more complicated problem. Adrenaline sharpened the mind.

She shouldn't be here. The hour was too late, the streets deserted. Shops had closed hours ago. Her purse lay on the ground, discarded, unwanted. The two men hadn't meant to rob her.

He needed to get her out of here, and shifted her higher against him in preparation to move. If she woke to find two dead bodies, she would likely become hysterical, and he wasn't in the mood to deal with that human emotion. Maybe the beauty's purse contained useful information. He scanned the ground for any abandoned items.

Something moved in the shadows. One of the attackers, his fingers curling.

Tightening his grasp on the unconscious woman, he stepped closer to the man, and with eyes used to the night, caught movement behind the man's eyelids.

He was awake.

Soren pulled his gun and sent the man back into blackness with a single shot.

He had to find out who or what these men were. Nothing should have come back that fast after tangling with him. Nothing ever had. He didn't like this, not at all, and cursing under his breath, pulled his phone from his pocket and dialed an all too familiar number. Only Gustav could sort out this mess and provide answers.

This was his corner of the small, smoky room. With a glass of cheap merlot in one hand, and a cigarette in the other, Gustav sat in the middle of pure bliss. Not a large crowd tonight, but it didn't matter. The rhythmic, heavy drumming of the music filled in the spaces.

As he took a long and soothing pull on his cigarette, an orange glow lit his face. He surveyed this hidden hotspot. Two men much larger than him guarded the doors, though their presence wasn't warranted. This place didn't have a name, which made it hard to find. Not that he was hiding, just indulging in his Friday night routine.

Friday was fight night here, and inside the cage, the house champion leaned lazily against the metal links. A tall man, even without the extra three inches of spiked black hair. He didn't speak as he looked through those gathered around, waiting for anyone stupid enough to step inside with him.

And there was Stupid, surrounded by his buddies, being slapped on the back by one and having his shoulder shaken by the other. Clearly, pumping up the challenger's ego. Nineteen, twenty at the most, the boy strutted inside that cage like he'd already won.

How wonderful, that brief moment when the champion took his first real shot and the challenger realized how badly he'd screwed up.

A muffled ring reached his ears as his pocket vibrated. Gustav took the phone out and flipped it open without looking at the caller ID. There were only two people in the world who called him.

"Yeah."

"You have a mess to clean up, my friend. I'm on Rue Daru," the man on the other end said, followed by a disconnecting click.

Gustav tossed the phone on the table and rubbed his hand over his face, smoothing his goatee. In the cage, the boy lay flat on his back, and the champion back against the links. He'd waited a week for this, and missed the moment that made him remember who he was and why he was here. He snagged his glass from the table and drank the contents down quickly, needing the wine to keep him warm tonight.

Gustav left, walking through the rain. He hadn't been far from Rue Daru, a short side street smack between Parc Monceau and the Arc de Triomphe. He'd known something was wrong the moment his weekly happy time had been shattered. Soren rarely came into Paris, and never called for help. This could be interesting.

———————————

Soren picked up the purse, a bit tricky to do as he held her limp body, but he refused to set her down, to let go of her. Besides, the only place to put her was in a puddle.

She didn't have much in her purse. He fished through the little thing, ignoring the English to French phrasebook, the lip gloss, and a small guide entitled City Walks: Paris (50 Adventures on Foot). Opening her wallet, he removed her license. The outdated picture showed her hair at an odd, short length.

Faith. Her name was Faith. How very simple, demure. Human.

She was still unconscious, but beautiful. No specific feature drew him. He just couldn't describe her any other way. And that alone made no sense.

Soren pulled stray pieces of her wet hair away from her face, smoothed it back with the rest. After he found the knot on her head, relief filled him. It did not bleed. She'd have a terrible headache, but she would be fine.

He cursed himself. This wasn't supposed to happen, not to him. How could he have been so stupid? He hadn't meant to frighten her. Should have taken the time to seduce her, to draw her in with sweet words and a gentle touch, making him easier to forget. He should be a distant memory, or at most, a story of a romantic encounter. But he'd craved a taste of her so badly he hadn't attempted to soothe her fears. Fear heightened the senses. She was likely aware she'd been bitten, and that was impossible to explain away.

Not in all the centuries he walked the earth had he ever lost control.

"Lurking in alleyways, Soren?" Gustav scolded from the shadows, his off-kilter French accent bending his words.

"Gustav. What took you so long?"

"When all you give me is the name of the street, you're damn lucky I'm here at all," Gustav said, stepping into the alley. His goatee hid his face, keeping him blended well with the darkness. "Open your eyes and throw me a number next time."

Gustav halted before the two bodies splayed across the cobblestones.

"Soren," he said expectantly. "Who are they?"

"I don't know. Both attacked her."

Gustav turned his piercing gaze to him, and then to the woman he held. "I can see why. I would. So what's the problem?"

Growling his frustration, he tried to shield the woman from Gustav's unhurried perusal. "They're dead. That might be a problem."

"All right, then. Let's see what we have." Gustav lowered himself to the ground in a quick, fluid motion, balancing on the balls of his feet as he examined the two men. The first man's face was bloodied and smashed. If he'd lived, it hadn't been for long. But the second... "You shot him?"

Gustav had every right to question him. Not only was this out of character for him, but the entire vampire race firmly disagreed with taking a life.

"That one started moving not long after he hit the wall." His tone was dark, accusing.

Gustav's focus shifted sharply to the men on the ground. With the injuries sustained, neither man should have been able to wake. He pulled up the first man's top lip. Fangs protruded, gleaming white. The man with the bloodied face was the same. Gustav touched the first man's cheek with the back of his hand, then the second.

"Both are very warm to the touch, even with the chilled rain working hard to cool their bodies," Gustav mumbled, talking more to himself than to Soren.

The heat should not be there. He silently prayed as Gustav lifted an eyelid on each man, checking for the color of the iris. Gustav shot to his feet, drawing out a short sword tucked under the folds of his coat.

"Not in my city," Gustav snarled with teeth clenched. And with the accuracy of one familiar with killing, he stabbed both men through the heart.

"They were..."

"Yes." Gustav wiped the thick, dark blood from his sword onto the shirt of one of the corpses. "It's been two decades since I've seen more than one in the same place, and nearly a decade since I've seen any of those red-eyed devils."

"I assumed they were Vampire. They look like us. Strange."

Gustav agreed with a nod. "They can appear either human or ghoulish, but the red eyes don't lie," he said as he searched the pockets of the fallen demons. Finding nothing more than cash, cigarettes, and a lighter, he stopped.

Soren was shaken, and though he tried to present a calm demeanor, his short answers and studying gaze would be enough to alert his friend that he had sunk very deep in thought. And that was due to either the demons, or the woman in his arms.

"And her?" Gustav asked, pointing a finger at the woman.

"She's mine." Soren pulled her legs up and cradled her. Now was not the time nor place to discuss what would be done with her. "We'll talk at your home."

He walked past Gustav, his precious cargo's limp arm swinging with each step.

"Very inconspicuous, Soren," Gustav said.

"Let's see how inconspicuous you are moving two dead bodies." He left the alley, and his friend.

———————

Faith looked up at the silhouette of a man curled over her body, his head barely blocking the raindrops from pelting her face. She was moving, her feet were not, and the city was sideways. The foreign world passed by her, the images coming slowly, as if she were seeing everything through someone else's eyes.

She was numb, her muscles from cold, her mind from shock. Her memories seemed intact, scrambled and hazy, but intact. She remembered being afraid of flying on the airplane, and the taste of the ginger gum that kept her nausea at bay. She'd been lost in the rain on the way back to her hotel. Then two men had trapped her in an alley.

Her shoulders and ribs shuddered with chills powerful enough to make her teeth rattle. She fought through it, lifted her head and look down at her hands.

"My purse." The words didn't come out right. Her jaw refused to open, and her lips had difficulty forming the simple words. She tried again. "Took my purse."

"I have it. You need to be warm and dry right now," the man said, keeping up his pace, never once looking down at her. By the sheer confidence in his husky tones, without a doubt, this was the man who had saved her. That intense look on his face was nearly the same as when he'd pulled the muggers off her, driven them into the wall. It was oddly comforting, at the moment.

Tall buildings, probably homes, surrounded her, swaying in her field of vision as he strode along. Light peeked through several arched windows, yellow and warm.

He entered one of the larger buildings as if he owned it and carried her past several numbered doors to the end of the hallway, where he started down a creaking set of stairs. Suddenly she feared falling down those stairs, but her shuddering muscles wouldn't allow her to hold on tighter. She closed her eyes and trusted him not to drop her.

After the last step had been left behind, she took a deep breath, opened her eyes, and almost wished she hadn't. The basement hallway was musty, and each bare light bulb they passed only revealed cracks chasing each other across the ceiling.

He stopped, pressed her against a green door as he fished for the doorknob with the hand supporting her legs.

"Put me down," she said, trying to help, and fully expecting him to drop her to her feet.

He fought with the knob until it finally gave and carried her inside, then kicked the door shut behind him. Dodging an old faded green couch with sunken cushions, he swiftly took her to the next room. She caught sight of a small bed and a green dresser with blue splotches where the paint peeled away before she was swept into a bathroom and set on the toilet as if it were a regular chair.

He left her alone in the bathroom while he rummaged through the dresser drawers in the other room, but returned quickly.

The light in the bathroom revealed him for the first time. Tall, but not towering, he stood in the doorway, rain dripping from his short hair. His straight and relaxed eyebrows followed the squared line of his forehead, giving him a very serious look.

He reached out, and she flinched. An automatic reaction, and unnecessary. His target hadn't been her. He set a pile of clothes on the sink between them.

"Get out of those wet clothes," he said.

She shook her head, her protest silent, but firm.

In a gentler tone, he tried again. "Look at your hands."

She did, but only because he didn't crowd her. Practically white, her hands shook badly.

"Dry yourself and change. You're safe here," he said, then shut the door.

She lifted the T-shirt from the top of the pile and held it up. A man's shirt, the words across the front French, but she didn't understand them. She set the shirt on the other side of the sink, and dug through the clothes. A thick pair of cotton socks and navy sweatpants, and beneath the pants, a towel. He'd given her a towel.

Smiling, she picked up the blue, fluffy thing and pressed it against her cheek. Never in her life could she remember being this happy to have a towel. Her excitement was misplaced, but she didn't care. She leaped to the door and twisted the small lock securely.

She stripped off her sweater first, dried herself, and then threw on the T-shirt. It was comfortable, and almost fit. She struggled to pull the wet jeans from her legs. The heavy fabric clung to her skin. When she'd tugged them free, she lifted the sopping mass of clothes from the floor and tossed them into the tub.

Leaning back against the wall, she steadied her balance as she yanked on the sweatpants and socks. The sweatpants were too long. She rolled the waistband down a couple of times, which would keep the hem from getting caught underfoot.

She caught sight of herself in the mirror and paused, not completely recognizing the woman looking back. Her mascara had decided to retreat from her lashes to give her those very lovely 'raccoon eyes' every woman dreaded, and rightly so. But it wasn't just that. Her face looked ashen. She must be much colder than she felt.

Holding her hair over the sink, she wrung out the water. What she wouldn't give for her hairdryer, a big Remington running full blast on high heat. She'd probably give up on her hair and point it at her feet. Leaning against the wall again, she tipped her head upside down and rubbed the already wet towel over her hair vigorously, drying it as best she could.

Her breathing came in short, labored bursts. As she stopped drying her hair and lifted her head, her vision darkened, and she let the towel fall.

Blindly searching with her hands for something solid, she fell against the wall with a thud and slid to the floor.

Chapter 2

———

PARIS

She lay on the bed before him, her small frame perfect. Soren had piled several blankets on her, helping her body keep its warmth. He gently repositioned her arms and pulled the blankets over her shoulders. This was the second time he'd carried her unconscious. She hadn't spoken yet. He was beginning to worry.

Not wanting to leave her alone, he picked up her black purse and sat back in the only chair in the room, silently praying the rickety thing wouldn't collapse with him in it.

He looked again through the few contents of her purse. She was without a doubt the most unprepared woman he'd ever run across. Holding up her license, he compared it to her. He shifted carefully in his chair. What was it that drew him? Vampires could be any shape, size, and skin tone, but each one had jet-black hair. And so did she. Since he'd been a fledgling, he hadn't been crazy over the color, but now that hers had dried, he wanted to bury his hands in that dark mass of hair.

What he wanted more, was to bite her again. And he could have her, do anything he wanted with her. She was his by law. He squeezed his eyes shut for a moment then stood and left the room, closing the door softly behind him, shutting her off from his sight. Soren shifted his shoulders, rolled his head from side to side, but nothing eased his restlessness. Thirst sated, he did not need more blood. Regardless, he seemed to want it. And he wanted it from her.

It must be a simple biological reaction, possibly rebelling from deprivation. Being a full grown male, he would require sustenance every six months. He'd been pushing a year. The events of tonight had made it quite obvious why feeding should be done every six months, despite personal reasons for avoidance.

If he were going to stay in that room with her, watch over her, he would have to find something else to do with his teeth.

On the counter in the modest kitchen lay a bowl of small, round apples. Thankful to have something solid to sink his teeth into, he took two.

The door opened and Gustav entered, having no trouble with the temperamental latch. Gustav spared him only a glance before beginning the ritual of returning his weapons to their proper places. He stuffed his gun into the silverware drawer, along with several small throwing knives that Soren was certain Gustav also used for meals.

"Eating me out of house and home again?" Gustav asked as he mounted his short sword on the wall behind the couch. A deadly decoration.

"I wouldn't be hungry if you hadn't taken so long," he said.

"Do you have any idea how long it's been since I've had to deal with these bastards? I'm lucky Geoff still has his van. I'd like to see you dispose of two bodies in under an hour." Gustav snorted as he removed his jacket, then walked past him, headed for his room.

Three solid seconds later, Gustav marched from his bedroom.

"Oh, come on. You put her in my bed?" he whispered harshly.

"Back off."

Gustav let out an irritated sigh. "What happened tonight?"

"I don't know." Soren looked at the door she was hidden behind. "I just wasn't thinking."

Gustav crossed his arms, unmoving. "You're always thinking. You've always got it all planned out."

"Not tonight," he said, avoiding his friend's steady stare.

"So when you said *she's mine* up there, you were being literal." Gustav still studied his face, his reactions.

"Yes. She knows what I am, what I took from her. I'm sure of it." He could not let a human wander the world with knowledge of vampires. To do so could mean the death of thousands of his kind. Their laws limited him to two simple choices. Keep her or kill her.

Gustav shrugged. "I could kill her if you want. Then it's not a problem anymore."

Soren glared at him.

Gustav's jaw dropped. "You're really keeping that bit of human."

"I can't explain it. It's been so long since I've fed, and I want more," he said, ignoring his friend's shocked expression and going to the door. "I need to think. Watch her."

He had enough to deal with right now, and explaining his thoughts and feelings to Gustav was not on his list.

"She better not wake up," Gustav grumbled.

Holding the door open, he paused. "Warn your lord about the demons."

"He knows," Gustav said, and Soren shut the door behind him.

The sharpness of the door closing sounded somehow final. Halfway up the stairs he stopped, fighting the urge to return. He didn't want to leave the human.

Faith. He didn't want to leave Faith. The more he thought of her, the more anxious he became. What if she woke? She didn't know Gustav, and might be frightened. If she became hysterical, his friend would probably shut her in the bathroom. It sounded completely preposterous, except for the fact that Gustav became irritable when something new was thrown his way, and tended to act on impulse.

He headed back down the stairs. She'd already faced two demons and his less than admirable attentions. One of Gustav's tirades would scar her for life. He opened the bedroom door and Gustav looked up at him, a smile curving beneath his goatee.

"Back so soon?" Gustav said in mock innocence.

"Get out."

"I see why you want to keep her, and why you crave her. She's stunning." His rich and mirthful laughter rang through the room.

Soren pulled the card key to Faith's hotel room from her wallet and shoved it into his friend's hand. "Go find her things."

"With pleasure," Gustav said with a cocky smile, and smacked the small wooden arms of the chair as he practically leaped out of it. "I can't really blame you—"

"Out," he snapped.

The springs in the mattress creaked, bringing her slowly around. After prying her eyelids open one at a time, Faith looked around the room.

She lay in bed, her head throbbed, and the dim light was bright enough to compound her headache with stinging darts of pain. She couldn't see much, but from what she gathered, the only thing to see was an odd wooden chair with some kind of canvas holding it together.

Again, the springs in the mattress creaked, but this time she was awake enough to realize she hadn't moved. Someone was sitting on the edge of the bed.

She tried to sit slowly, not liking the vulnerability of lying down in a strange place.

"You should lie back down," a man said.

She sat anyway, and he covered her shoulder with a large hand, pressing her to the mattress.

"Listen, buddy, I want to sit up. So leave me alone and let me figure it out, or help me up," she said, struggling against his hold.

The hand on her shoulder changed directions, and he gently pulled her to a sitting position. He might have moved slowly, but it felt like she'd been pitched forward. She had to squeeze her eyes shut to stop the room from spinning. Palms flat on the mattress, she braced herself, simply breathing.

"You passed out again. How are you feeling?" he asked.

When she looked up at the man, she recognized him instantly. He'd saved her life, and carried her down here after she'd passed out in the alley. She'd never passed out before. Yes, being robbed had been scary, but after he'd shown up, she hadn't feared for her safety. Except when...he'd bitten her.

"You...you're..." Her voice shook, even as she kicked the blankets at him and backed against the wall. "Get away from me."

That sudden movement had been a very bad idea. She leaned back against the wall for balance and clutched her head with both hands.

"You hit your head pretty hard. Do you remember what happened to you?"

"I don't have amnesia." She snapped her mouth shut, holding back a whimper, then whispered, "A mild concussion, maybe."

The volume of her words rattling around inside her head hurt badly. She wanted very much to lie down again and sleep for a whole day, but messing with her equilibrium to get her head to the pillow was something she dreaded at the moment. Stillness seemed to work the best right now. She opened her eyes enough to see him through her eyelashes. Satisfied that he hadn't made a move toward her, she asked quietly, "Why am I here?"

"Because it's safe here."

"Where is here?" She gave it another go.

"A friend's home."

"Wow, are you cryptic." She wasn't getting any water out of this rock, and gave up.

"Habit," he said, shrugging one shoulder as if apologizing.

"Well, it's a bad one." With her fingers, she searched out the sore spot on the back of her head. If there had been any doubt in her mind, the bump under her fingertips revealed that she had definitely hit her head. "Why didn't you just leave me in the alley?"

"Do you remember what happened?" His voice had changed with this question, and she swore she heard a touch of hope in his words.

"Boy, do I. You bit me. Bit me!" She'd gradually gotten louder and she had to catch herself. "You should have left me."

"If you didn't remember, I could have. But you know what I am," he said, lowering his head. "Even if I had wanted to let you go, I couldn't. There is no other choice. Now you will stay with me."

Her mouth hung open in surprise for a moment before she snapped it shut. "I'm not staying with you."

He leaned closer, gaze narrowing on her. "Leaving you to those two monsters would have been the only way of avoiding me. And if I had, death and dismemberment would've been the very least of your worries. I say again, I have no choice."

A chill shimmied up her spine, made her shiver. The problem was, she believed him.

As frightening as those men had been, the man sitting before her was the one who had bitten her on the neck. It had stung, searing, before her vision dimmed.

"Have I really been kidnapped by Dracula?" she whispered, watching his lips, afraid of what was behind them.

He raised his eyebrow, and then cleared his throat. "Dracula is dead, and was not one of our kind. My name is Soren. And I am vampire, if that's what you're asking."

She stared at him now, unable, or maybe unwilling, to stop. This man certainly wasn't the pasty, caped creature she automatically associated with vampires, nor did he look eternally youthful. And she supposed his aged look threw her the most. His skin had a natural tanned tone, and when coupled with the grooves across his forehead and the smile lines bracketing his lips, he looked like a worn thirty-five-year-old man. How could a regular man be a vampire?

The bedroom door swung open. A short man stood in the doorway, nearly hidden by her large blue suitcase. He tossed it on the floor.

Soren sighed. "This is Gustav."

"I wish you would have let me kill her. This thing weighs a ton," Gustav said, then his gaze fixed on her and narrowed. He turned to Soren. "You gave her my clothes? This isn't getting any better. Get her dressed and out of here."

"We're going," Soren assured him, his mouth twitching as he fought a smile.

"I hate people," Gustav grumbled, then caught sight of the splintered door. "Hey, what the hell happened to my bathroom door?"

She certainly wasn't going to take the fall for that one. As Gustav looked between them angrily, she discretely pointed to Soren.

"Forget it, I don't want to know." Gustav left, throwing his hands in the air.

Soren lifted her suitcase and set it inside the bathroom. "I thought you might want your things. We'll be leaving soon, so bathe and change your clothes."

Despite her pounding head, she was up and across the room in an instant. It didn't seem like a smart thing to try a vampire's patience.

Soren watched as she tried several times to get the door to latch right. She barely got the thing to close even as she used her weight to pull it into place. After she'd passed out, he'd nearly torn the door off its hinges the instant he'd heard the solid thump of her body against the wall. Yet again, he was struck by her human weakness.

He'd caught her in time to keep her head from smacking the floor. Funny, how a bump on the head and overexertion caused a human to pass out.

He would have to be drunk or nearly dead to lose consciousness. Even the women of his species were amazingly resilient. Faith was vulnerable, and he needed to shelter her. Which he shouldn't want to do. Shouldn't even think it. He had other, more important things to attend to.

Demons ran free in Paris.

Their red-eyed faces filled mind, but an image of Faith took over, soaking wet and terrified of them. He stood and began to pace the room, rubbing the back of his neck as he moved, anger growing.

He had to stop remembering her fear, and that the demons had touched her. It made him furious, volatile. Gustav's casual request to kill her nearly sent him over the edge.

And when he took her home? It had been so long since a human had been brought into their world. His whole life was being rearranged in an evening, because of one woman.

_____

Faith knelt on the floor, popping the metal latches and lifting the lid of her suitcase. She might be able to get out of this. Soren was a vampire. He had several obvious weaknesses. She was not the kind of woman to tote around garlic, holy water, and wooden stakes. Frankly, that kind of woman should be committed. That left sunlight and crosses. She had no idea what time it was, but she retained some hope of being able to use the sun to her advantage.

Dear Lord, she hoped she'd brought her tiny diamond cross necklace. She thought somehow she hadn't, but dug through the powder blue satin pockets anyway. Her fingers touched the small jewelry box, and she pulled it free and flipped the lid off. Earrings. Thick gold hoops, and thin silver hoops. No necklaces. Why did she have to be so practical?

Letting out a heavy sigh, she sat on the floor rather ungracefully. Elbows on her bent knees, she stared down at her suitcase, defeated.

The fake blue leather was so familiar, the plastic handle cracked and worn. She'd packed light, the trip kindling the hope of many things...to find some unique jewelry, a sexy pair of casual shoes, and maybe a place to stay. It would be nice to live in France. Or anywhere else. Home hadn't felt like home in...well, she wasn't sure if she could technically classify it as being home in the first place. Her two-bedroom house belonged to her father. He'd bought it for her birthday last year.

A week later, her mother bought furniture for her living room. And so it had continued. Nearly fifteen years after their divorce, they continued their fight with each other through her. She'd begun to hate every gift dropped on her welcome mat, yet another gift from her mother.

This beautiful blue suitcase in her closet had started to look appealing, almost like an oasis. She'd kept shutting the closet door, pretending it wasn't there. After all, an oasis was an illusion, a mirage.

Then one day she'd come home to find that her mother's gardeners had planted spiral topiaries and boxy hedges right over her favorite white peonies. Faith hated spirals and hedges. If her mother had bothered to take the time to carry on a full conversation with her in the last five years, she might know that. Faith was through with letting others plan her life. She'd wanted out, and had finally understood if she didn't try to find that oasis, she'd never know if it were real.

So here she sat on the floor of a bathroom with nothing to lose. This wasn't exactly the oasis she'd envisioned, but at least there was water in the form of one very good-looking vampire. It could be, and almost had been, much worse.

———

Soren sat in the rickety chair, tipped his head back and took a deep breath. Everything here was in sad shape, especially that sorry bed he'd barely remembered from his last visit. He'd always wished he could change things for Gustav, though Gustav wouldn't want anything to change at all.

His friend was a rarity. What his people called a Stalker. He was vampire, but dedicated to the death of demons and to the protection of vampires and humans. Stalkers walked the night above, struggling to find shelter from the daylight, living as humans.

Soren had chosen a different way of life. He was a Guardian, his sole duty to protect his lord, and the people of his lord's city. A peacekeeper. He guarded his people from within the city. They defended their race in their own way, though he would be the only one ever recognized for his efforts, rewarded with a plush home and the respect of his people.

Gustav would never have any of that. Vampires held no respect for Stalkers because of their love for killing demons. True, the only good demon is a dead one, but murder is still murder. And had always been punishable by immediate execution.

Stalkers were criminals running free in the world. At least, most vampires held that opinion. Gustav was a good man, a good friend, and Soren really didn't care if he butchered every last demon single-handedly.

Exhausted, Soren released a heavy breath and let his thoughts of politics and friendship fade away. The soft sound of water splashing and a sweet flowery scent wafting from the bathroom started to relax him.

The water drained, and the hum of her hairdryer created a pleasant background noise. It conjured memories of her damp hair in his hands. It had felt like satin slipping over his fingers.

It had been so very long since Soren had lived with anyone, let alone a woman. Although he kept a busy schedule, his social skills were somewhat lacking. Always had been. He likely was more apprehensive about this situation than she was, and going home with a vampire was about as strange as it got, for her.

The door rattled once, twice before popping open. Faith nearly tripped on her way out, but righted herself and tried to gently prop the unstable door against the wall.

Her black boots peeked from beneath her blue jeans, and anything he'd planned to say fizzled into nothing as his gaze drifted upward. No longer rain soaked and disheveled, her hair fanned over her shoulders. Her shirt softly hugged her hips, following the curve of her waist. A turtleneck covered her lovely neck to her chin. Laughter burst from him.

"What's so funny?" Faith demanded.

"If I wanted you, blood, body and soul, that bit of cloth would not hinder me," he said with a smile.

Her hand rose halfway to her throat, but she caught herself, dropping her arm. "I'm still wearing it."

"Suit yourself." He still smiled at the notion of using a piece of fabric for protection.

She sent him a sideways glance as she went to the bed and placed the clothes she had been wearing in a neatly folded pile. She leaned forward, and her hair slid across her back and draped over her shoulder. Long and brushed smooth, it fell just below her shoulder blades in a soft vee. No choppy layers, no wispy pieces falling over her eyes.

Perfect. Lovely. He imagined what it would be like to sweep back all that soft, sweet smelling hair, to bury his face in it as he fed.

He rose, and in two steps stood behind her, lifting her hair to his face, drowning in the scent of flowers. She gasped, but he clenched his fist tighter, not willing to let her go.

Chapter 3

═══

PARIS

Half afraid of what he would do, she closed a hand over his fist behind her head. Traitorous excitement buzzed through her. His body seemed to curl around her, and the possessive, sexual heat rolling off him shocked her to her core.

Footsteps approached, and Gustav's impatient voice broke the tension. "If you don't want to stay through the day, you'd better get going."

The warmth of Soren's body evaporated, making her shoulders shake once with a sudden chill. Hiding her reaction to his touch, she quickly combed her fingers through her hair. Funny, but it felt like Gustav had intruded.

Soren met him in the doorway, their hushed conversation apparently none of her business. She couldn't make out a word. Faith took the opportunity to duck back into the bathroom, retrieve her suitcase and haul it to the door. Soren stood, glaring at the keys dangling from Gustav's hand, and she paused.

His legs were parted in an almost challenging stance as he argued with Gustav, arms tightly crossed and jaw clenched. She smiled. The argument must not be going Soren's way. He looked angry, and Gustav's voice rose steadily.

"Do it your way and you'll fry in the dawn light, you stupid, stubborn bastard. And then she's stuck with me." He motioned to her, though Soren didn't turn his head her way. "Hysterical women aren't sensible, and you know it. One way or another, she'll be dead along with you. If a demon doesn't get her, I'll have to."

Soren growled, but didn't say a word.

"Hey, nobody needs to kill me. I'll go with you," she piped up. Her fate *would not* be decided by two hotheaded men.

"Yeah, but this idiot wants to walk to Balinese," Gustav said. "Which would be all fine and dandy, but you've been knocked in the head, and the only thing you'll do is slow him down, killing you both in the process."

Gustav gave her one of those looks that screamed for help. Well, she'd give it a shot. She was all for not dying. Sinking onto the edge of the bed, she quietly asked, "How far is it?"

"Far," Soren bit out.

"I don't think I could keep up with you," she said, throwing some girly weakness into her voice. "And what if I pass out again?"

"Listen to her, Soren. Neither you nor I know how many more demons are out there right now. If you stop to fight them, you waste time. And what if you're injured?"

After a long moment of contemplation, Soren leaned on the doorjamb and tipped his head back, tense in his defeat.

"Damn," he whispered, squeezing his eyes shut.

"What's the matter?" she whispered to Gustav.

"He hates cars," Gustav supplied.

"That's it?"

"He's never liked them." Gustav shrugged, apparently quite familiar with Soren's quirks.

"I thought all guys loved cars. Were you in an accident?" she asked, though she didn't expect a response.

"Unreliable hunks of metal," Soren muttered, snatching the keys from Gustav's hand.

"He hates progress in general," Gustav answered with a smile. "The only real exceptions I've ever seen are indoor plumbing, his guns and his phone. He hates his phone, too."

Soren picked up her suitcase then curled his fingers around her elbow. Without a goodbye to Gustav, he pulled her along behind him and right out the door.

Soren tossed her suitcase in the backseat of the rusty two-door car, and as he stepped aside for her to take the passenger seat, spotted a woman's shoe on the sidewalk. No woman alive would leave a single shoe behind. Alive being the key word.

The smell of blood hung in the air. Demons. They stole lives in mere moments, leaving only a damaged, empty body behind. Hatred rose, swelling like a storm ready to break, destroying all in its path. He controlled it, at least for now. Blind hatred did nothing but dull the senses.

Faith stood at his side, oblivious, a stranger to his world. He had no time to educate her. She knew what manner of being he was, but nothing of the vile creatures thriving in the darkest blackness of night, held at bay by a single streetlamp.

He didn't hear it, didn't see it, but something had shifted in the shadows. He captured her delicate wrist and pulled her behind his body, shielding her.

"She looks tasty," someone said from the shadows.

"You'll never know," Soren said.

Faith leaned closer to him. She must have finally become aware of the danger.

Footsteps moved steadily toward them, and he dropped his head, studying the sounds, blindly memorizing every movement ahead of him. The demon's steps echoed off the building. He wasn't facing it.

He'd backed Faith up against the car, and suddenly the sound shifted, coming from behind them. Gun already pulled free, he turned. Cupping the back of her head, he pulled her tight to his chest. But the creature was fast, and before he found it in the dark, a slicing pain tore across his wrist. The gun dropped from his hand.

"Not so easy now, is it, vampire? With no weapon, how will you defend this little morsel?"

Soren pushed Faith back against the car, keeping her far from the demon. A knife glinted in the creature's hand. The demon twisted it, waiting for an attack. He would have one.

———

Faith couldn't watch his fist connect with the man's face. A few more punches, a muffled snap, and then silence.

She looked from the crumpled man to Soren. No one had ever pounded a man into the pavement to keep her safe before. She didn't know the rules for something like that. Did you thank the man, or scold him? Somehow she felt like she ought to do both.

The man on the ground lay motionless, the light catching something wet beneath him.

"You really hurt him. I think he's bleeding." She squinted as she bent down, getting a closer look in the dim light.

"It's not hurt, Faith, it's dead. Get in the car," Soren said, pushing her into the passenger seat and shutting the door.

Dead. She looked at the man's face one last time through the film of dirt on the car window.

Red eyes stared blankly back. Red eyes.

Numbly she was aware of Soren getting in the car, putting it into motion, and taking out his phone.

"Gustav, there's a body where you park your crappy car," he grumbled. Muffled yelling came through on the other end of the phone. "Just take care of it."

The more she thought about this whole situation, the more frightened she became. Here she sat in a car with a killer. Okay, so he had saved her life twice, but he'd just killed a man with his bare hands. That might be a normal, everyday thing for a vampire, but it had shaken her, badly.

And if he truly was a vampire, then what other creatures were running loose in the world? And was her attacker part of that mythical group? People didn't have red eyes, and Soren's eyes weren't red. What did he kill?

"His eyes were red," she said aloud, still looking out the side window.

"I know."

"His eyes were red," she said more firmly. If he was avoiding it, it meant something.

"Faith—"

She smacked the dash. "Damn it, Soren, why were his eyes red?"

"It was a demon," he said, not meeting her glare.

She stared at him, her jaw slightly unhinged, then nodded slowly.

"Of course he was. Why didn't I think of that?" The pitch of her voice rose several notches. "Great, there really is a hell."

"There is, but these creatures didn't come from hell. Demons are simply another species of human, as is vampire." A smile turned the corners of his lips upward slightly.

"Right, and how many species are there?" Her fingers tapped the armrest.

"Four. Human, vampire, demon, and wolf."

"Wolf? As in Werewolf? I didn't see that in the brochure." Faith glanced out the window, and muttered, "While in Paris be sure to see the damned."

"None of us are damned. Well, the wolves are, but that's what you get for pissing off a witch. What's left of them reside somewhere outside London. We tend to stay away from your kind. Humans are unpredictable at best," Soren explained, his focused stare glued on the road.

"Then why do you live in Paris?"

The car was creeping to an intersection. What the heck was he doing?

"I don't exactly live in Paris. We all have to feed and we've a better chance of being forgotten if we take what we need from tourists. Tourists get a thrill and we get the nourishment our bodies require for proper healing. This is the city of love, after all," he said in a tight voice.

"So you romance them, suck their blood, and then leave? Good God, no matter what species they are, men are pigs."

"You won't hear an argument from any one of them," he said, taking the car carefully around a corner.

"Hey, I'm arguing here." She waved her hands at him, but he didn't look away from the road.

"Yes, but if I romanced you, you'd change your mind."

"Right, let me just scoot over and make room for your male ego," she said, fixing her gaze out the window.

What would it be like if he romanced her? She'd never been truly romanced, at least not by her standards. Could she hold her ground? She watched him from the corner of her eye.

Not a chance. With him, she might as well throw in the towel from the beginning. He was handsome, in a refined manner, and considerate. He'd held the car door open for her. Okay, so he'd shoved her in after he opened the door, but still, he got two points for the effort. And another two points for those muscles.

She liked the way he made her safety his personal mission. When he'd let his inner barbarian free to kill the demon with his bare hands, she hadn't been afraid for herself.

Traveling in silence, the scenery passed at a slow pace. He drove like a grandpa with his hands precisely at ten and two, hunched over the wheel as if reading some find print on the windshield.

She stifled a giggle, disguising it with a cough.

He couldn't have been going over forty miles per hour. Better than walking, but nearly a joke when behind the wheel. With no other cars in sight and the city far behind, driving still seemed quite the feat for him. His white fingers wrapped around the wheel tenaciously. Poor guy.

This was the first touch of insecurity she had seen from the vampire, and it wasn't much. He remained in complete, slow control. "Do you want me to drive?"

"No," he said sharply.

She didn't try again. He could have his macho trip, and burst a blood vessel in the process. His call. At this speed she would have plenty of time to relax.

Chapter 4

———

BALINESE

Soren left the car at the edge of a dense forest, and led her to the entrance of a very narrow path hidden in the trees. He pushed through the thick foliage ahead of her, clearing a crude trail. They stepped over trees, some fallen, while roots of others reached above ground. This entrance must not be used often.

"I thought we weren't going to walk," she complained as she pushed another branch away from her face.

"It's not a long walk," Soren said, weaving around a sapling that almost reached his height. "You're keeping up just fine."

"I know I can keep up, I'm just worried creepy things are lurking in the forest." She copied him, dodging the tiny tree.

"There are no demons here, I promise you."

"I meant spiders, but thank you. Now I can't decide which is worse, eight legs or red eyes." The hairs on her nape prickled as if something followed her, and she quickly closed the gap between them.

He laughed quietly at her sudden skittishness. "Like I said, there are no demons here."

The trees thinned, and as the path ended, Soren stopped. Down a gradually sloping hill ahead of them lay an old chateau. This was not her idea of a vacation hot spot. The chateau had no aesthetic appeal. It was a fortress with high walls and narrow windows. A tall structure, its squared center rose higher than the rest of the block-like architecture.

"Wow, you live here?"

"I do," he said with pride. "This is my home. This is Balinese."

He took her hand, helping her to keep her balance. The descent was steep, and she wasn't used to this kind of terrain, but his sure footing and confidence chased away any concern.

The ground leveled out, and Soren settled his hand across the small of her back, guiding her. It was for the best. She couldn't stop staring at the chateau and wasn't paying attention to where she walked.

"Faith, my world is not like yours. Keep quiet and stay close," Soren warned in a whisper.

She nodded, still lost in studying the large and looming chateau. Soren pulled her through an arched entry, the door deeply inset to shelter visitors from the weather. He didn't open the door, and instead he turned his face toward the dark corner to his right.

"Steffen," he said with a short nod.

A man came out of the shadows in a single step, his sad blue eyes peering through stray pieces of long, straight hair.

"Shall I request an escort to lead her to the dungeons?" he asked, his fangs visible.

"No, she stays with me." He pulled her closer to his side.

Steffen's eyebrows shot upward, his curiosity clearly piqued.

"Is there something you want to say?" Soren challenged.

"No, sir, absolutely not," Steffen said, but his gaze remained on her.

"Wise choice, but if you do not stop looking at the human, I'll correct the problem for you," Soren said, low and deadly, and Steffen immediately shifted his attention back to Soren.

His angry words made her shake involuntarily with a sudden chilling fear. This was real. There were two vampires next to her, and she could only guess at how many more were inside. Despair grew inside her, icy and unsettling.

"I need a cross," she mumbled, but after her words drew the questioning attention of both vampires, she took a step back. At least, she stepped back as far as Soren's rather solid arm allowed.

"Steffen," he said, holding his hand out to the other vampire, who drew a rosary from beneath his shirt, and passed it quickly to him. Both men faced her, seeming truly concerned.

In his hand was the very same rosary that had lain around Steffen's neck. She opened and closed her mouth several times before deciding on the question least likely to get her killed.

"Isn't that supposed to hurt you?" she asked Steffen.

"Want to see the scar?" he answered in a bland, bored tone.

"Enough," Soren warned.

Steffen snatched the rosary back from him with a snort. "It doesn't hurt."

"But...but I thought vampires would, well..."

When she couldn't finish her sentence, Soren supplied the answer. "It's a myth, the same as holy water and garlic. We invented them to make humans feel safe. Not one of them works."

"Crap," she said.

"Scheming to kill me with a cross, were you?"

"Thought about it," she admitted.

"I'm sorry I spoiled your plans. The attempt would have been...interesting." His eyebrow jumped slightly, and unmasked curiosity flashed on his face and in his twitching smile.

Goodness, the man was a magnet. She didn't have any interest in peeling her gaze from him.

"Personally, I love garlic." Steffen tucked the rosary under his shirt.

"That explains a lot," Soren said as he opened the door and guided her through it, away from Steffen and further into the chateau.

"Real nice! Pick on the guy with no social life," he called after them.

In the dim light within, she made out the comfortable furnishings and a large fireplace, but beyond that, the room felt eerily quiet and abandoned. After Soren took her by the arm and steered her sharply to the left, she understood why. That grand room was apparently not traveled.

He opened a tall door, the wood thick and heavy on its well-oiled hinges. Beyond the door was a kitchen with a pale stone floor and walls reflecting the moonlight from the window. Each step echoed off of the stones as they walked through the room. It felt empty in here, too.

He opened a door on the other side of the kitchen, revealing stairs that likely led to a cellar. He'd saved her life earlier, and it stood to reason he'd keep her safe. She'd trust him for now, and stick close.

Soren led her down the stairway. It turned sharply to the right once, twice. On the far wall a torch hung, shedding light over old, dusty barrels and bottles that likely hadn't been touched in years.

"Through here," he said, opening another wooden door, this one with wrought iron hinges and handles.

He gently pushed her through and guided her to the right, down a long corridor. Gray, bare walls seemed to continue on forever, interrupted by evenly spaced sconces. After only a dozen feet or so, he steered her sharply to his left into a corridor she hadn't realized existed.

Her steps stuttered to a halt. Thick, richly colored tapestries bordered in red lined the walls, covering the stones. The scenes depicted battles, coronations, graceful ladies on horses, and knights jousting before castles. Soren urged her to move again, and she did, but slowly. There was too much to absorb.

She reached out, touched the tapestries. Soft, beneath her fingertips. Someone had taken very good care of them. The detail of the nearly eight foot tall masterpiece was impressive. She dropped her hand to avoid the narrow black and gold table between the tapestries, only to become lost in the rich red carpet covered in wispy, elegant white vines and buds. It was beautiful, like walking through a cozy castle.

Never would she have guessed that a species only wakeful at night would appreciate such beauty and color. Of course, she hadn't expected Soren to have an aversion to cars either. He wasn't the vampire she'd assume, but common sense told her she should fear him. He'd killed three men since she'd first seen him, and he was technically the only one who'd succeeded in harming her tonight. Somehow, that didn't matter.

He cupped the back of her neck, his fingers gently climbing higher until they grazed her pulse. His full focus straight ahead, he matched his pace to her shorter stride.

His touch drifted over the very same spot where he'd bitten her, but it no longer hurt. In part she'd worn the turtleneck to cover what she'd assumed would be an obvious vampire bite, but there hadn't been one. When she'd checked her neck in the crooked mirror hanging in Gustav's bathroom, the wound had already healed. He hadn't truly harmed her. Maybe that's why she didn't fear him.

The hallway ended, opening to a balcony rimmed with black, wrought iron fencing. A mass of thriving vegetation drew her closer, but the vision of clean blue water rippling gently beyond enthralled her.

"This is beautiful," she sighed, heading for the railing.

"You have a lifetime to look at water. I have more important things to do right now." He took her arm and steered her down yet another corridor, this one was blue, royal, and plush.

Ahead of them a door opened, and a giant of a man stepped into the hallway. She moved back against Soren, allowing and expecting him to shelter her.

"Bareth," Soren called.

The broad shouldered man only grunted as he strode heavily toward them.

Soren blocked Bareth's escape. "I need a favor from you."

"Oh, come on," he protested.

"Five minutes. Just watch her," Soren said, and then ducked into the same doorway Bareth had just exited.

"You suck," the man grumbled, plopping down on a bench.

He'd left her. What the hell? She was alone in a strange place with a mountain of a man. She couldn't take her eyes off him. He was larger than Soren and probably stronger. That he'd sat down should have made him less intimidating. It did not.

Bareth lifted his arm, and she flinched. He merely rubbed his belly. Her nerves settled, but the simple movement had already kicked her heart rate up a notch, making her jumpy.

He studied her as well, and she took a step back. Suddenly, almost as if the man couldn't think of anything else to do, he smiled. A lopsided, hesitant smile that showed his front teeth, including fangs.

"I...I think I need to sit down," she said, her voice barely a whisper as she sank down onto a long bench. It strangely resembled a church pew. How appropriate. She felt like praying.

Vampires. The word hadn't really bothered her until Soren had left her alone with a man who might be a fair match for The Hulk. Now she had questions, and more than a few concerns. Were humans their only food source? Would she be passed to whoever needed blood? What if Soren let this man have her? How much blood would he need? Would someone always be sucking at her neck? No, that was ridiculous. Eventually she would be out of blood. Then she would be dead.

Despite the panic rising to choke her, the tears stinging her eyes, she held in her terror. She might not have anything or anyone to live for at the moment, but she certainly wasn't ready to die.

Bareth sat in the pew opposite her, hands folded over his belly, head resting on the wall. He might be large and strong, but he didn't look like he'd run far without becoming winded.

This could be her only opportunity to escape. Taking a deep breath, she stood, her legs shaking slightly beneath her. All she had to do was reach the entrance without meeting anyone along the way. She pretended to look at the tapestries and turned her back to the vampire.

He slouched deeper into the pew, and she sprinted down the corridor, not looking back. She rounded the corner, came out onto the balcony, and bolted up the red corridor. No footsteps fell behind her.

She dashed through the heavy door and closed it quietly behind her. Through the wine cellar and up the stairs she ran, past the kitchen. There she stopped to catch her breath, but only for a few seconds.

Edging closer to the wall, she walked slowly. Since Soren had broken down and taken the car from Gustav, aversion to sunlight was a true weakness for vampires. It should be near morning now. Would the guard they'd met on their way in be seeking shelter? She hadn't passed him. He was either gone already, or still at the gate.

She peeked out into the foyer. It was quiet ahead of her. Slowly, she opened the door to the alcove where the guard had been posted. Nothing.

A sweet, cool breeze touched her heated face, adding to the surreal feeling of her escape. She took one step, two steps. When she wasn't stopped, she ran again, the forest and her freedom getting closer.

———

Soren shook his head. Navarre was the only lord he'd heard of who did not conceal his rooms in some obscure corner of his city. Oh, no. It was quite obvious the lord of the city lived here, by the royal blue colors covering this hall and the frequent visitors who came to his ever-open door. Were he a poor ruler, the blatant advertising would be a bodyguard's nightmare.

Lord Navarre Casteel, however, was a great ruler. He saw Balinese as his child, nurturing her, watching her grow and prosper. Once the lord knew of the danger to Balinese, as any father would, he'd protect her fiercely.

He'd known Navarre for centuries, and they had the best kind of friendship. Informal. Soren closed the door behind him, not bothering to throw the lock. The Captain of the Guardians had lectured Navarre dozens of times about the dangerous habit, and he had yet to listen. His confidence bordered on arrogance. Then again, that was part of what made him great.

Moving through the large foyer lined with white columns, Soren made his way to the next room. More often than not, Navarre could be found in his personal library. The walls on the left side of the room were lined with inset shelves holding hundreds of books, caged in by doors decorated with a golden crosshatch design. A desk and study table stood in the midst of the books, currently unused.

"Soren," Navarre greeted him then dropped his gaze to his work, his overly long hair falling forward.

"My lord," he replied, stepping into the library.

"What is it today? Rats in the wine cellar, problem with a student, or have you come for a game of chess?"

Navarre sat as usual beside the fireplace with a book in hand. It would never be leisurely reading, but something of vampire history. His friend was always studying his own people. Once, he'd caught Navarre searching for any loopholes in their judicial system. Even now, his lord remained glued to the oversized book.

"I fear this is a great deal more serious than rats." Soren sat in the chair opposite and waited patiently for him to finish reading.

Navarre looked up at him, brows knitted in thought, then put the book aside. "You don't look well. Go above, find a soft woman to sink your teeth into."

"That was the plan. But I encountered a bit of...difficulty."

"Difficulty?" Concern stretched across his lord's features. "That is not a word that should be in your vocabulary, Soren."

"I wish very much that it wasn't." He rubbed the back of his neck and sucked in a deep breath. "I found two demons attacking a woman in the streets of Paris."

Navarre simply sat in the same relaxed pose. Slouched, his knees spread and elbows on the arms of the royal blue chair, he remained still.

"Another attacked me as I made my way back. Three total," Soren said.

Still Navarre did not move. After a long moment, he finally spoke. "What does Gustav say?"

Soren hadn't mentioned to anyone that he still spoke to Gustav. How much his lord knew about his city, his people, and the world above continued to amaze him. "Gustav hasn't seen any demons in a full decade. He didn't take their presence well. Needless to say, they are very dead."

"Alert the Guardians and have several scouts sent into Paris."

"I'll find Captain Savard immediately," Soren said as he stood.

"The council will meet in one hour, and you will be there," Navarre said, leaving Soren able to do nothing but nod.

Walking to the door, he forced his footsteps into a normal, even pace. He didn't like this urgency he felt. The threat of demons must be setting him on edge. That, or Faith. He feared for her safety, but there was no reason to, not here. Yet he could not deny that he did.

Closing the door to Navarre's rooms behind him, he looked down the hall. Bareth lounged on the pew. Alone.

"Where is she?" he asked, frantically looking around.

Bareth shrugged. "Running."

"And you didn't stop her?"

"That's Steffen's job." He stood, stretching his arms over his head.

"You lazy, good-for-nothing..."

Soren sprinted down the hall, following the only path she would know to take.

Chapter 5

—

BALINESE

A shout rang out behind her, and her heart lurched but she didn't turn. Soren chased after her, without a doubt. She had no illusions of outrunning him, but resisting the impulse to fight for her freedom had been impossible.

Soren's thick arm caught her high around her waist, jolting her to a halt. He spun her around to face him. The anger seething from him gave her the urge to bolt, but he'd trapped her, and she wasn't going anywhere.

"Do you have any idea how lucky you are? Guardians have full permission to kill on sight any human running from the city!" Soren roared.

The volume of his scolding voice kicked her courage into gear. "Stop shouting at me."

"I can't. I'm yelling at you. And it feels a lot better than thinking about what could have happened."

Without another word, he took her arm and towed her back to the city. She gauged the distance between the city and where he'd caught her. She hadn't got far, and her hopes of freedom died under his tight grasp.

As he pulled her through the entrance, fear tightened her gut and she stumbled. Steffen stood off to the side, utterly still and watching them in silence, sword drawn and ready. He appeared more than willing to use his sword on her.

Soren took her back the way they'd come. They rushed through the red corridor, but this time he stopped and opened a door, ushering her inside. He closed the door, paced in front of it a few times, then stared at her.

"Where are we?" she asked.

"My home."

Awkward. She stood in the middle of an angry vampire's living room waiting for him to yell at her.

"Our world is peaceful," he finally said, his voice deep, sounding as if he restrained himself from shouting at her. "Our world is simple. And yet somehow you manage to do one of the few things guaranteed to get you killed."

"I could have made it to the woods." She shrugged.

"On the very unlikely chance my Guardians had not seen you, what would you have done? Run to Paris?"

"No. Just to the car," she said with a smug smile. "You left the keys in the ignition."

"I hate that damn car," he growled at the ceiling before turning on her. "Had you escaped, you would have been reported missing and hunted down. It's not something I would have the power to stop. Too many lives area at stake. You will live here, or you will die. You are mine, Faith. And when you are with me, when you are in Balinese, you are safe."

Anger swelled, burning. Arms stiff by her sides, fists clenched, she marched to him, stood toe-to-toe. "I don't belong to you. You might be forcing me to live here like a prisoner, but I am not yours."

"This is no game, Faith. You belong to me so that you may live," he said as he studied her face. "I want you to live."

Biting her bottom lip, she looked away. His reasons hadn't been invalid, but they made it difficult to get over her anger. Quietly, she said, "I wouldn't tell anyone."

He took several deep breaths before looking straight at her. "It wouldn't matter. I can't risk the lives of thousands. No vampire will. If you escape, you'll be killed. Swear you'll never run from me again."

"I won't, but I had to try. Wouldn't you?" She wrapped her arms around herself.

He turned away from her and rubbed his jaw. "I can't give you an answer. I have no notion what I would do if I were in your position. I never will."

She nodded. "So where do I live?"

"Here. My home is yours," he said as he walked to the bedroom. Soren stopped as he reached the threshold, his gaze lingering on her as she stood in the middle of his home. "I'll be gone for an hour or so. I have a meeting."

He disappeared into the bedroom. She didn't follow him, not wanting to invade his his personal space. A laughable concept, she supposed, since she now lived smack in the middle of it.

She heard water run, but not the shower. Then hangers shifted. He stepped into the living room, and she was pleasantly surprised. He'd exchanged the black T-shirt for a dark blue collared shirt. If not for the harsh scowl on his face, she might have teased him on how nicely he'd cleaned up.

He glanced her way as he passed her, but didn't pause. "Stay here."

The door slammed shut, and she didn't waste any time. She planted her butt in the nearest chair and rubbed her eyes, pulling her hair off her face. The attempt at refreshing herself helped, but only a little. Her tired body needed rest, and rightly so. It was morning, and the whole night had been a series of traumas, discoveries, and traveling. She pinched the bridge of her nose briefly, easing the tension that had settled there.

She opened her eyes, and straightened in the chair. On the wall before her, a battle-ax hung at an angle, held up by two large hooks, and to its left, a painting with a lady and a knight on a stairway. Rising, she slowly turned, taking it all in as if in the middle of a museum.

The paintings, large and vibrant, had been separated by weaponry. The innocent romance in several paintings countered the harsh edge the unsheathed weapons gave the room. Or maybe the danger was in the man who lived here.

The bedroom took on a similar medieval theme, but here she found no weapons. This room held several works of stained glass art. One imitated a window, the view a lush scene of rolling hills and bright green trees. Beautiful.

Ending her tour was the bathroom. Elegantly designed, the white and gold stripes ran from floor to ceiling. She skimmed her fingers over the burgundy shower curtain as she walked out. He wasn't a slob. That was nice. Everything seemed to be in its place. She'd expected the bathroom and kitchen to be trashed.

Stopping short, she counted the rooms suspiciously. Three. No kitchen or dining room. They were missing.

Of course! Vampires wouldn't eat at a table. It would be far more convenient to bite the nearest neck. Great. Now she needed a distraction from the thought of blood drainage.

Snooping through Soren's bureau drawers and under the bed, she didn't find anything to give her a hint about him, or even something to occupy her time. She found nothing. No TV. No radio. The man didn't even own a chessboard. A home with this kind of decor could absolutely use a chessboard.

"I'm going to be bored for the rest of my life," she said, sighing as she flopped onto the bed.

Soren hadn't been called to a meeting before, and would be perfectly happy if he never saw one again. The council consisted of good and wise men, and he understood their necessity, but this sort of thing was not his cup of tea.

It didn't appear as if Captain Savard enjoyed these meetings either. Three seats remained empty for guests and emissaries, but the captain quickly gave up his seat for him. No surprise there. The man did not like being stagnant.

Captain Savard leaned against one of the wooden pillars bracing the walls. No one would suspect that he was the second most powerful man in Balinese. His stature bordered on the definition of short, and unlike the strapping Guardians, he was leanly muscled. His long black hair would have touched his jawline if he didn't keep it swept back from his face. Other than sideburns, he had no facial hair and appeared to be a young man in his early twenties. While his appearance didn't necessarily intimidate, his reputation did.

With the captain abandoning his chair, Soren now sat beside Navarre, who presided over these meetings, his word final, even over the council's decision. Vidor and Julian indulged in the idle conversation of noblemen, seeming not yet aware of his arrival.

Five men resided on the council, and these two had been hand chosen. Vidor Wesleyan was the last of the oldest aristocratic family, and had been on the previous council belonging to Navarre's father. Julian had later been appointed to represent the nobility. Kind, fair, and sensible, Julian remained a favorite among both common man and aristocrat. Navarre chose well when he'd added him to the council.

Bareth, the city's High Justice, had yet to arrive. Like the lord and captain, Bareth's presence was required because of his prominent title.

The double doors burst open, Bareth easily filling the open space.

"And there he is. If you can't make it here when you're called, how the devil do you get to the arena on time?" Julian teased, hands folded neatly before him.

"It's my job to be there," Bareth countered, flopping into the chair next to Soren.

"Yes, but it's your job to be here as well." Vidor tried, and usually failed, to keep Bareth in line.

"This isn't nearly as fun as the arena," Bareth grumbled, then cast a quick smile at Navarre. "Why are we here, my lord? And why is Soren here?"

"He discovered something which needs to be brought under consideration. Soren, speak what you know," Navarre prompted.

Every man in the room waited for him to open his mouth, and he shifted in his seat. No matter what he said, or how he said it, this conversation had a minute chance of going well. "I went above this night and found two demons attacking a woman in an alley." As expected, a ripple of murmurs and sneers followed the word *demon*. "I encountered another on the way home. The last knew I was vampire and targeted me."

"Before we go further, let me inform you that Captain Savard has doubled the Guardians at the gate and sent a few scouts into Paris. We will know soon if more are out there," Navarre said.

"This is dreadful." Julian combed his fingers through his long, wavy hair, pulled it away from his face.

"What happened to the woman?" Vidor asked, his eyes narrowing on him.

"The woman lived and knows what we are. She's mine." What he'd wanted to be a clear statement had ended up more of a declaration.

Bareth chuckled. "She's a runner, is what."

"You didn't try to catch her." He jabbed his finger at Bareth. "You watched her run down the hall."

"A human attempted escape? Navarre, we cannot allow this," Vidor protested.

"She didn't get far." Soren, instantly guarded, shifted his attention to Vidor. "You have the entire city to meddle with. Stay out of my personal affairs."

Vidor's sharp stare drilled into him, and the nobleman puffed out his chest, ready to battle.

"No human will leave the city," Captain Savard said, ending the argument. "This is not an issue. Move on."

"Soren," Julian said, calm and collected, though seeming surprised by his odd behavior. "You're getting as serious as the good captain. Be at ease. We would not take her from you."

"The demons weren't after the woman, were they?" Vidor asked, suddenly more anxious than agitated.

"It seemed so at first, but they prefer females. I can't be certain." Soren shook his head. "Why would they want her for anything other than a meal? She's a tourist. She knew nothing of our city or people until tonight."

"That doesn't mean she didn't stumble into something," Julian suggested.

"I doubt it." She'd seemed so upset once he'd told her what she'd assumed had been a man had truly been demon. "She didn't notice their red eyes until I killed the last one. She didn't recognize the creatures, only saw them as cruel men."

"But if they are after her, more might have followed you here." Bareth rubbed his chin, pondering his own suggestion.

"Not likely. I took a car," he admitted, which drew several curious glances.

"Leave her to the demons. Let them have her," Vidor said with a dismissing wave of his hand.

"She's human." Soren pinned him with a sharp and angry stare from across the table.

"Exactly, she's human. The world is full of those expendable creatures. One life for all of ours is a fair trade." Vidor nodded decisively, as if his logic would be considered supreme rule.

"She's innocent." Growling, he stood, tensed and ready for a fight. He only waited for Vidor to start one. Faith belonged to him, and he would protect her, from his people if necessary.

Navarre cleared his throat, and Vidor and he stilled, awaiting the lord's judgment. "Vidor, you are right. One life is more than a fair trade to save this city."

A chill washed over his face as the blood seemed to drain away. Nausea tugged at his stomach. The shock of what Navarre intended to do numbed him. "My lord, you can't possibly mean to—"

"Easy, Soren," Navarre interrupted, waiting until he sat before continuing. "I would gladly give up one life to keep my city safe. However, we have no proof the demons are truly after her. It could be coincidence. All we're doing is speculating. Both attacks happened only streets apart. Hardly convincing evidence demons intend to harm her, and only her. More than likely they were pack hunting, just as they used to before we wiped them out. And Soren, you were present at both attacks, but we have yet to say the demons may be after you."

Grunts of agreement rumbled through the room.

"I don't want to lose sleep and lives over demons again," Vidor said. "My apologies, Soren. It is not your human woman setting me on edge, but the presence of these demons. They should have been hunted to extinction years ago."

In complete agreement with Vidor this time, he nodded. He often forgot Vidor had been alive when demons ran unchecked, and humans hunted both vampire and demon. Granted, being of noble blood, Vidor had never fought in those wars. Though war, on any level, would have made an impact on every vampire, no matter their station.

"Soren?" Navarre leaned forward, his long hair falling over his shoulder, reaching to where his elbow rested on the arm of his chair. "You said she didn't recognize the creature as anything other than man until she saw its eyes. Explain."

He hesitated, loathed being the bearer of very bad news. "They looked human, my lord."

"What?" Vidor leaned back against his chair, his body slack and his eyes wide, horrified.

"Except for the red eyes and fangs, the demons could have passed for human men. No discoloration or sunken skin. Worse, they didn't act mindless or desperate. One spoke to me, and he was completely coherent," Soren said, shaking his head in disbelief. "More unbelievable, and what I dread to say out loud, is that it seemed normal to Gustav. Unwanted and hated, but normal."

"They might be a different breed of sorts," Julian offered.

"Very possible," Navarre nodded.

"The creatures should be eliminated," Julian said.

"What say you, my lord?" Bareth's booming voice filled the room. "Shall we wipe them out once more?"

"I'm not yet certain we have a problem. They could have been stragglers from another city, another country. I won't send men out to hunt them, not when Soren likely killed them all." Navarre looked around the table, waiting for argument. "We will wait for the scouts to report."

"Just like Soren to get a hold of those demon bastards first." Bareth chuckled.

"You never leave anything for us old men sadly out of practice, do you?" Julian said with a smile.

"If I weren't High Justice, I wouldn't get a chance to swing a sword. It's why I took the job. Needed my exercise. At least that's what Gretta says," Bareth said with a shrug of his broad shoulders.

"Gretta's right." Vidor laughed. "You are getting rather thick in the middle."

"My woman's always right." A knowing smile spread on Bareth's face.

"Of coarse she is, Bareth. That's why you mated her," Navarre smiled.

"Captain, you've been quiet," Vidor said, glancing at the captain who had stood in silence.

The captain sucked in a breath, sounding as if he were exhausted and looked not at all thrilled with being singled out. "I'm here solely to gain information for the protection of Navarre and the entire city. I have no opinions."

"You're on the council. Your opinion counts a great deal," Vidor pushed.

"I do as my lord commands." The captain's calm level stare made Vidor hastily end his pressuring.

"Good to hear," said Navarre. "Captain, inform the Guardians at the gate of these new creatures. Meeting adjourned."

The councilmen exited the room, but Soren stayed. After everyone except Navarre and the captain had left, he finally asked the question burning for release. "What if they are after her?"

"I won't give up a female, even if she's not vampire. She's here now, and she's yours. I refuse to negotiate with demons. But should we find more, the council will be demanding a hunt." Navarre reclined in his chair, though he didn't relax. "Captain?"

Silence hung in the air, and for the longest time, Soren thought the captain wouldn't answer his lord.

"When you hunt things down, you unavoidably miss one or two." Captain Savard spoke slowly, deliberately. "One man with a vengeance is a dangerous thing. Imagine two."

What he'd witnessed surprised him. The captain did have an opinion. He'd merely saved it for Navarre.

Navarre nodded. "Agreed. Do what you can, Captain. I have no interest in revisiting our past."

At his words, the captain left to no doubt do what he did best. Defense.

"Thank you," Soren said. "Her safety means a great deal to me."

Navarre stood. "She's not the hysterical type, is she?"

"No." Soren blinked a couple times as he processed the question. "Not at all. In fact, she seems rather levelheaded."

"Good. Bring her to last meal. I'd like to meet her," Navarre said as he walked from the council room, not waiting for Soren's response.

Time to go home. With Faith's future now certain, he breathed easier, but each step toward home hit the ground urgently. She was alone, and even though Steffen guarded his door, he didn't trust her.

He rounded the corner, and immediately asked, "Did she run again?"

Steffen shook his head, already walking away. "Nope."

Half expecting her to bash him in the head, he opened the door cautiously, but encountered only silence. The lights had been left on in every room. He didn't see her, or hear her.

A stinging lump rose in his throat. If she hadn't run, then where did she go? Had something happened to her? The thought terrified him more than he cared to admit.

He entered his bedroom, and the tension fled from his chest. She'd kept her word.

At the scene before him, he shook his head. Faith lay sprawled on her stomach across his bed, her right arm folded over her heart, left arm pressed somewhere between her stomach and the comforter. The sight of her hair completely covering her face, her nose peeking out, almost made him laugh out loud.

Regaining his composure, he covered her with a blanket. He should have turned around then, walked away, found the couch and let sleep take him. Instead he remained there, smiling.

Something was wrong with her, or maybe him. He rarely lost his temper, and never with a woman. But he had with her. When he'd seen her running across the grass, his heart nearly stopped with fear. Steffen had been close by, ready to kill. Yet he remained thankful Steffen's shift hadn't ended. No one else would have recognized Faith.

Then he'd yelled at her. He hadn't meant to raise his voice, but he couldn't control himself at the time. She put him on edge. He'd been insanely jealous of Steffen simply speaking to her, and ready to fight a council member over his right to keep her. She unhinged him.

Soren controlled the urge to brush her hair from her face. He wanted to lie next to her and pull her against his chest, and just hold her. As strange as it sounded, sleep held no appeal if he couldn't have her beside him.

He couldn't recall standing over a woman as he did now, wondering if she needed anything he could provide. Did she need another blanket? Had she gone to sleep hungry? What kind of daily rituals did she have? Would she mind if he lay beside her?

With a growl, he closed his eyes, and turned away from her. His instincts screamed at him, demanding he bind her to him as his mate. Those internal impulses always had a reason, a solid need for being present, but this time he couldn't understand them. Faith already belonged to him. According to his laws, he could do anything he wanted with her, but it wasn't enough.

If he mated her, she'd have to become vampire. It would be an all or nothing deal. She couldn't be turned without being his mate, and she couldn't be his mate without being turned. This kind of thing should only be considered if...

Most vampires mated, binding themselves to someone they loved. Rarely, though, did a vampire find their true mate. Histories and legends said the only thing more potent than the calling of the sun was the pull of your other half, the one meant to save you from death and give you life.

Staring at Faith, he couldn't believe it possible. Not after all these years, not with a human.

Placing his hand on the mattress, he leaned closer, wanting to somehow test his theory.

Faith woke with a start as the mattress dipped, and rolled onto her back. She peered up at him, but her eyelids remained mostly closed, as if she were unprepared for the bright light of the room.

"What is it? What's wrong?" she mumbled, still half asleep and groggy.

"Nothing, get your rest." He'd forced out the words, unsure if he lied to her, or himself.

She flopped back onto her stomach. Readjusting herself on the bed, she tucked her hands under her body. Before long, her breathing became even.

Soren pulled a thickly cushioned chair near the bed and watched her sleep. The possibility she was his one true mate could not be denied, but he would ignore that hope and be pleased with reality. She chased away the loneliness in his life, even if fate hadn't handpicked her for him. Caring for her gave him a new purpose, a different reason to live.

Chapter 6

———

BALINESE

Soren woke in his chair near nightfall to find Faith staring at him. She sat cross legged on the bed, her hair mussed and the blanked wrapped around her shoulders.

"You were gone a long time."

"I know. The meeting ran long." He hadn't expected her to wake first. Her alert gaze threw him off-kilter.

"About the demons?"

"Yes, and you don't need to worry about them."

Her eyebrows pulled together as she processed his words, then she nodded slowly. Projecting a steady resolve, she said, "I need you to answer a question."

Sitting straight in his chair, he rubbed his hands over his face, hoping his brain would wake up enough to function. "What do you want to know?"

"Are you the only one who can, um, bite me?" she asked as she tucked her chin under the blanket.

For a moment, he could do nothing more than blink at her. "I won't allow another to touch you."

Her shoulders dropped, and she no longer looked directly at him. He didn't know her well enough yet, and had difficulty interpreting her actions. Had his words brought her disappointment, or relief?

"It's freezing in here," she said, a lame attempt at moving past the topic of biting.

He'd turned down the heat when he'd gone above. Feeding always left him warm, and he hadn't noticed the chill.

"The thermostat is there on the wall." He pointed, then stretched in the chair. "Turn the heat up to wherever you like. We'll be heading out soon. The shower is all yours. By the time you get out, the room should be comfortable."

Faith got out of bed, her clothes rumpled and wrinkled. Her first stop, the thermostat. She didn't waste any time pulling specific items from her suitcase. Instead, she dragged the whole thing into the bathroom.

Soren waited patiently for the door to latch, then pulled his clothes from the dresser. After he'd changed, he went back to the dresser and kept pulling out his clothes. He stacked the bottom two drawers full, leaving the top two empty for her. The clothes that rebelled against being shoved into their new home would be tossed in the laundry basket and dealt with later.

He didn't have any experience with someone else living in his home and didn't know what would make her comfortable. Clearing some of his space seemed like a good first compromise. He pulled the empty drawer out slightly for her to find it herself.

Faith finally came from the bathroom, and he called out from where he waited in the living room, "I'm in here."

She fluffed her hair as she walked into the room.

"How's your head?" he asked.

"Not bad. The dizziness stopped, and today I just have a dull headache." She sat across from him, trailing her fingers over the burgundy crushed velvet loveseat. "This is beautiful."

"Thank you. It belonged to my mother. She had a ridiculous weakness for settees, and my father happily indulged her. Every few months I switch this one out for another in storage." What should he make of her pleasant attitude? She'd been attacked, abducted, and now permanently kept. That she was so calm seemed odd.

"I can't wait to see what the next one looks like," she said, a quick smile crossing her face.

"You seem rather at ease with your captivity, especially after your attempted escape." He leaned forward, elbows resting on his knees, and awaited her explanation. She was acting strange, and he made a mental note to watch her closely.

"I still don't agree with you. I'm not yours. But I do accept that I'm stuck here with you."

"What makes you give in so easily? Have you no backbone?" She flinched at his words, and he regretted them, but not enough to retract them.

"My backbone shows up when I need it, and right now, I don't. I can't leave. Why try? I'd rather make the best of what I have."

"No family?"

She shrugged, leaving his question unanswered.

"Then why run?"

"You left me alone with that big scary man," she said, pointing at him. "I saw his teeth, and he's the same as you. He could have easily killed me before you came back."

"He'd never hurt you. I forgot how intimidating he could be." Damn. He should have considered she might fear Bareth. Her courage, though, made him smile. "I'm sorry he frightened you, but honestly, you did better than most when they first meet Bareth."

"Really? Why? Is it because he's so large?"

"In part, but mostly because he's an excellent swordsman with the brute strength to back his blade. He's also a Viking, a heritage that tends to make even vampires fear him."

"I didn't think Vikings could be vampires," she said, shaking her head.

"There are more of us than you would expect," he said, and she gaped. Eyes wide with wonder, tempting lips parted...amazement looked good on her.

"You're a Viking?"

He nodded. "A descendant."

"Well, that explains the..." She pointed at him, then brought her hands to her shoulders and spread them wide.

"Genetically speaking, that has more to do with my father being on the large side, but thank you for noticing," he said with a teasing smile lighting his face. "Bareth and his wife have been friends of mine for a long time."

"Someone married him? Brave woman."

He shook his head. "Lucky woman. Bareth is a good man, a good protector, and a great father."

Soren opened his mouth to speak again, but a knock at the door stopped him. A glance at the clock, and he had a good guess who would be here this early in the night. He popped open the door.

"Elin, how are you?" he asked the willowy vampire. Long wavy hair tumbled over her shoulders, framing her angelic face and hiding the beading over the top of her frothy blue gown.

Like always, she refused to answer. "You're back."

"It's nice to be home," he said with a short nod.

"Is tomorrow too soon?" she asked.

"No. Tomorrow is fine. Wait," he said, stopping her as she began to turn away. "Elin, can I ask a favor?"

"Anything." She sounded pleased he'd asked, and more than eager to help.

Soren cleared his throat. "I need a gown."

"Why?" she whispered, eyes wide as she leaned in.

He stepped aside, giving Elin a clear view of Faith sitting comfortably in his home. Elin's expression changed from curiosity to surprise.

"Just for tonight. I don't have time to find something suitable for her," he said.

"Okay. I'll leave one here while you're out." She looked between them suspiciously before turning away.

"Elin solved one problem for me," he said to Faith, clapping his hands. "The second problem is you. I have things to do today, and since I need to be certain you won't run again, you'll go with me."

"I said I wouldn't run, and I meant it." For him to think she made a habit of lying really got under her skin. Faith took a deep breath.

"I'm in the business of not trusting people. Forgive me if it takes me some time to trust you." Soren opened the door, waiting for her to join him.

She swept past him, and walked beside him through the red corridor. Could she blame him for being suspicious? Not really. They were practically strangers. "What exactly is it you do? And come to think of it, what is your name?"

"Soren Rayner. I train young men in the art of combat and defense," he said, steering her right when she would have continued straight.

She studied his profile. What sort of man took on such a thing as a day to day job? "I can honestly say you're the first I've met in the profession."

"I'm certain I am." He smiled, stopping at a door and holding it open.

She brushed past him and paused to take in the size of the training facility. The door on the left looked like an entrance from a locker room, and the gym equipment on the right side of the room had been arranged in a maze. Thick mats lined three walls, and a wide variety of weapons hung on the fourth.

"Gawk and sit, please. My students will arrive shortly," Soren said, pointing out a short bench.

She hadn't realized she'd stopped until his voice prompted her to move. Collecting herself, she sat as Soren headed for the next room.

Head resting against the padded wall, she took in the medieval weapons. The variety ranged from broadswords to crossbows, and above them, lances hung like trophies. Did Soren know how to use these?

He walked past her without checking on her, or if he had, she'd missed it completely. He'd changed into a white T-shirt and loose, black pants with two stripes running down the outsides of his legs. He looked more human this way, like a regular guy going to workout at the gym.

Several young men entered from the adjoining room, acting every bit like wild teenagers. Laughing and pushing each other across the room, they calmed once they stood before Soren.

"Are you ready to begin?" he asked.

"Yes," the seven boys said in unison.

"Good. Today I'm teaching you to use your eyes. Keeping them open and being aware of your surroundings will save your life," he said, his gaze moving to rest on each boy. "All eyes stay on me. Another man is in the room. What color is his shirt?"

The boys shifted their weight from foot to foot, but no one spoke.

"Am I telling the truth? Is a man in here? You don't know, and if you don't know, how can you be certain there is no threat on your life? Not one of you can give me any description. If it were a demon, you'd all be dead." Faith held her breath as Soren pointed at her. Seven heads turned her way, their displeased teacher behind them. Gearing up for a lecture, by his expression. "You've completely missed the fact that you walked past a woman."

She lifted her hand, waving her fingers at them, though she didn't smile. She'd landed them in trouble, but understood the importance of this lesson. Maybe if Soren had trained her to pay attention better, she wouldn't be here now.

She hadn't expected awareness to be the lesson of the day, but it made sense. Soren excelled at catching details. She'd seen him fight above, witnessed him track the demon outside Gustav's home.

Those poor boys still looked startled to see her alone on the bench, but as Soren barked out directions, they scrambled for their swords, eager to begin practice.

For over an hour she sat in this same spot, watching him wield a great deal of patience with the boys. The gangly youths took uncoordinated swings at their partners, and a time or two, she bit her lip to keep from giggling.

They got an A for effort, but clearly some weren't cut out for this kind of thing. Talented or not, Soren worked with each one of them.

After their practice ended and the boys left the room, he approached her, a smile tugging at his lips. "I thank you for controlling yourself. A woman's laughter would crush their fragile egos."

"Were those some of your better students?" she teased.

He gave her a brief smile. "They've only been training a week, and they're still green. It's what happens when aristocrats want to play at being Guardians. The next group, however, are seriously training."

"I see," she said, more of an automatic response, than one of understanding. She guessed every culture had a military or police, and it only made sense for vampires to have their own version.

"Do you need anything?"

"No, I'm fine." Stifling a yawn, she stretched. He nodded, leaving her to prepare for his next class.

Vampires, as a species, were born with strength. She'd assumed the ability to fight would have come naturally. Though after observing the first set of trainees, she'd quickly changed her mind. They desperately needed a teacher, even for those unable to join the Guardians. Directing their strength was a necessary lesson.

Male laughter sounded, and five young men came through the door, not much older than twenty. This group seemed more confident than the first, and the three in front strode in with their chests puffed out. Shaking her head, she smiled. Men were the same everywhere. When in front of their friends, they all acted cock-of-the-walk.

The two trailing the main group, however, remained separate. Their quiet and reserved behavior didn't hide their friendship. Both men glanced at her in a head to toe sweep. A tremor shook her shoulders. She'd just been studied and judged, she felt it in her bones. After they turned to Soren and she was no longer on their radar, she sunk back against the wall, the tension easing from her gut. She crossed her legs, settling in for another long training exercise.

As soon as she moved, the largest in the group of three stopped and glared at her, dark hatred shining through his eyes. She shrank away from this menacing man's glower, at least as far as the wretchedly solid wall allowed.

"You don't belong here," he sneered, revealing his fangs.

"But I—"

"Leave." He reached for her, and she had nowhere to go.

Chapter 7

BALINESE

Faith opened her mouth to yell for help, but Soren was already there. He hooked his arm around the man's neck from behind, and threw him to the floor, where he landed flat on his back with a heavy thud and a grunt.

She hadn't truly been in danger here, but still his shoulders remained tense, his focus sharp. And she couldn't take her eyes off him. He hadn't acted like this the first time he'd saved her, or the second. This had nothing to do with protecting a woman. What he did now was pure male possessiveness.

Seeming disoriented, and looking angry, the young man scrambled for an escape. Soren gripped his shoulder and drove him back to the floor.

"You can't do that to Tarmon. His father's a nobleman," his friend objected.

"Then the first lesson of the day is for you, Cutler. Not everyone fights fair." Soren had no problem lecturing Cutler as he kept Tarmon pinned. "Meaning, few give a damn about noble blood, and won't waste time verifying your lineage before spilling it from your veins."

"The second lesson." He shifted his gaze from man to man, making certain he had their full focus. "When protecting your loved ones and family, don't fight fair. Nothing matters except victory."

Faith held her breath as he looked down on Tarmon and pressed his hand around the man's throat, almost daring him to move.

"And the lesson to you, fledgling? Never touch another man's woman," Soren said, low and lethal.

"Sh-she's not marked," Tarmon stammered once he finally took in enough air to speak.

"Not marked?" He never looked away from Tarmon. "It matters not if a woman is marked. She always belongs to someone whether he is a lover, a mate, a father, or a brother. If a man perceives her as his, he'll fight like the devil to defend her, to protect her and keep her. You would not survive such a fight. Have I made my point?"

"Yes," Tarmon rasped.

Soren let go of his throat and left him to gain his footing by his own means.

"Enough talk. Draw swords!" Soren shouted.

His gaze swept over her, no doubt making certain she hadn't been hurt. She mouthed *thank you*. He gave her a nod then turned and shouted orders, once again occupied with training.

She leaned her rigid spine against the wall, waiting for her breaths to come evenly. She should have known she wouldn't be welcome here at some point, and being in the middle of such a volatile confrontation made her want to stick to Soren's side like glue.

The tension didn't leave her, and from what she saw, he had no relief either. He looked wound tight. His previously smooth, patient gestures and movements now appeared choppy, as if he were irritated.

Soren left these men no room for errors. He was stern, his approach different from what she'd seen earlier, but it worked because these men fought well. They didn't require direction, and battled continually for nearly an hour.

The fighting finally ended. Ready to drop with exhaustion, the young men dripped with sweat. Soren hadn't even been easy on the two who had no part in attempting to eject her.

With only five men, he had participated fully, sparring with each man at least once. He'd done everything with them and he merely breathed deeper. Could he truly be this remarkable, or did endurance come with the vampire package? She had a sneaking suspicion he worked hard on a daily basis.

"We're done here. Get out of my sight. Titus. Dyre. Front and center." Soren waited, and after the others moved from earshot, looked between the two men standing before him. "Neither of you confronted or questioned her, though women are not allowed in this room. Why?"

This would be interesting. If women weren't allowed in here, no wonder they'd taken offense.

"You were already here. You saw her," Titus answered.

"And therefore must have a good reason for allowing her to stay. It's not our place to question you," Dyre added.

"Right, and wrong. I did know she was here and I do have good reason, but you shouldn't assume your elders are aware of what goes on around them. You have your own minds, use them," Soren said.

"We did, and had no intention of speaking our minds in front of everyone," Dyre said quietly.

"So say it now," he pressed.

She leaned forward, hands wrapped around the edge of the bench. Turning her ear toward them, she strained to catch every word.

"We saw how you looked at her." Titus had lowered his voice, following his friend's lead.

"And how was that?"

Titus and Dyre shared an uneasy glance, reminding her of children, each one waiting for the other to take the fall.

Dyre stepped up and answered, "Forgive me, but what I saw left me with the distinct impression—"

"You want her," Titus interrupted. "The way you look at her is pretty clear signal she's yours. And she's human. Two and two equal she just got here and you can't, or won't, leave her in your home alone."

"End of discussion. To the showers, men," Soren said, effectively dropping the subject and covering the glint of surprise that had crossed his face.

After numbly blinking several times, Faith pretended to inspect her fingernails. He hadn't denied his attraction, but instead of trudging through an awkward conversation, she chose to feign ignorance.

She stood, stretching her tired body. She'd sat in the same position for hours, and now her muscles craved motion.

"Are you done?" she asked as she speared her fingers through her hair and lifted it off her neck, piled it on top of her head.

"No. One more class, then I'm done for the day." His attention drifted to the locker room and the approaching men. "Sit."

"Don't worry, I can't run away from you. My legs feel like jelly," she said, lifting her heels off the ground in an attempt to revive her circulation.

Soren glanced at the locker room again, then back at her. "You need to sit now."

"Don't bully me just because you've been doing it all day with them," she said, hands on hips.

Three men walked in, curiously eyeing her as she faced off with Soren. Game over, at least for now. A man with a wounded ego would be hell to live with, and she had to live with him, so she sat, relishing the confusion on his face.

She crossed her legs and smiled sweetly at him, leaving Soren nothing to do but join the men. Unlike the awkward boys and young men she had seen earlier today, these three warriors commanded the room. In the midst of such strength and power, Soren fit perfectly.

"Nero, where is Steffen?" he asked.

"He's sleeping off the dawn," Nero said quietly, and dipped his chin for a brief moment.

What did it mean for someone to sleep off the dawn? When put in the context of sunlight being bad for vampires, it didn't sound like a good thing.

Soren nodded, stretched the tension from his shoulders and carried on, not allowing his obvious worry to interfere with his job.

"Men, I'm damn tired of toying with fledglings. Please, I beg you, show me no mercy," he smiled, his challenge thrown down.

The man with the narrow face and dark brown eyes gave a short laugh, acting completely unmoved by Soren's plight. "How can we show you no mercy if we struggle to keep our feet beneath us from your blows?"

"Not interested, Flynn?" Soren asked though it didn't sound like a question. Maybe Flynn's protests were a normal occurrence.

"I'll take on our good trainer," Nero said. "There are two females in my home driving me mad. I need the outlet."

"Brilliant plan, Nero," Flynn said, his kind eyes the only thing belying his rough exterior. "You wear him out, then Sampson and I might just stand a chance."

"Oh, no," the larger man said, leaning against the wall. "I'm staying right here today. I'll join in when I'm needed."

"Sampson can hang back. I'll take on both of you," Soren directed, pulling off his shirt as he walked toward the broadswords.

Faith covered her mouth, but the soft feminine gasp had somehow escaped. His shirt hadn't hit the ground yet when he stopped and looked straight at her, a devilish smile curling his lips.

A shocking jolt went through her chest and landed in her stomach. For the first time, she saw his desire for her shining through his eyes. It absolutely thrilled her, and she didn't understand why.

"Miss, could it be that our Soren is to your liking?" Flynn asked as he absently rubbed his nose.

Hoping to avoid the question, she ducked her head. She certainly did like him, and if they caught a glimpse of her warming cheeks, they'd have their answer.

"Of coarse she likes me, she followed me home," Soren said lightly, sending her a quick wink as he tested the weight of the broadsword.

The men chuckled, and Faith covered her face, her hands cool against her heated skin. She couldn't be more embarrassed. They must know that as she was in their city, Soren had bitten her, and she would be required now to live with him. Any vampire would make that obvious connection, but these three total stranger pointed out something she hadn't fully admitted. She was attracted to Soren.

When she peeked at him through her fingers, he'd already turned to his men, leaving her the freedom to examine him more thoroughly. How could she not think of him in a purely carnal way as he strutted around like some modern, bare-chested barbarian? No woman alive could see those hard-earned muscles shifting beneath his skin and not conjure up a naughty fantasy or two.

The heavy clank of swords startled her, dissolving her daydreams. Nero and Flynn moved in immediately, an intimidating pair of predators. They targeted Soren. They approached in unison, even deflecting blows meant for their partner. These two men had worked together often.

The other classes consisted of lessons and direction, but these men practiced the unpredictability of battle. They had no problems using a sword, or their heavily muscled bodies, to gain the advantage.

Flynn was quick, his strikes sharp and precise. Soren avoided them, leaving himself open to Nero's calculated assault. Flynn had a swift sword arm, and Nero, keen strategy. Though they impressed her, Soren possessed both skills and more. He had Flynn disarmed and on the ground, all in a handful of minutes. Not a big surprise.

His focus now turned full force on Nero. With Flynn taken out, the swordplay moved at a slower pace, and she had an easier time following the movements.

Nero shifted his tall body, either chasing Soren or forcing him to follow. Soren took caution, but when Nero suddenly changed direction, his blade grazed Soren's arm.

"Soren!" she screamed as blood dripped down his arm. Nero turned to her, and Soren took advantage quickly, shoved him hard enough for him to lose his sword as he landed.

She watched helplessly as Sampson appeared from nowhere, stepped between Soren and Nero. She smacked her hands over her mouth, refusing to let another sound escape.

Sampson swung hard and connected with Soren's sword, the heavy metallic ring filling the air. Soren's blade hadn't hit the ground yet when Sampson drove his body against him, sent him sliding across the floor on his back. Blood was now smeared down his arm.

Faith stood, already in motion, intent on reaching Soren. That is, until he laughed.

"It seems I can still teach you old dogs a thing or two. When fighting, ignore women or send them away. They're a distraction and could cost you your life," Soren said as Flynn reached out and helped him to his feet.

"True." Sampson gave him a broad smile. "But I'd still rather keep mine close."

"That's because she's a pit bull. I'd rather fight you than her any day," Flynn said.

"I'll tell her you said so," Sampson replied, walking away.

"I think he's really going to tell her," Flynn told Nero.

Nero shrugged. "I warned you about opening your mouth."

Discussing Sampson's wife and Flynn's big mouth, the men exited the room. She'd been caught up in their battle and had completely forgotten it wasn't real. Twice she'd embarrassed herself.

Making his way back to her, Soren snatched his shirt from the floor and pulled it on. A solid heat settled beside her on the bench, but she couldn't look at him, not yet. Maybe if she kept him talking he would forget she'd been afraid for his life. "You're training them to fight like those last three men. Why?"

Soren nodded. "A rare few of them will become Guardians. Guardians are what you might consider law enforcement."

"*Right*. So if I break a law, one of these guys will come running at me with a sword?"

———————

"Pretty much." Soren laughed. "I hadn't thought of it that way, but you're right."

"You've got a long way to go with the first group. Good luck," she said.

"Most don't make it through the first class. Others train for years before I'll consider recommending they become one of us. Our best Guardians were in the last group of men. Sampson is the lord's personal Guardian. Nero and Flynn are Council Guardians, and Steffen is our Gatekeeper."

"So they show up to knock you around?" Faith asked sweetly, smiling.

"They do, and enjoy it greatly." He couldn't believe how happy she seemed. Is this what life would be like with her? He'd do almost anything for a daily dose of her gentle teasing and playful smiles.

Yet Tarmon had frightened her. The relief on her face and clear appreciation of him when he'd come to her aid had been proof.

Soren stood, headed across the room with a purpose and opened a glass case that held a small arsenal of knives fixed on the far wall. He removed one, and returned to her side, spinning the blade slowly in his hand. The weapon was beautiful and deadly. Etched flowers covered the gold hilt, continuing their trail over the sharpened blade. He placed the knife in her hand, and she looked at him, eyes wide.

She tried giving it back, but he closed her fingers around the hilt. "It's yours."

"I don't know how to use this. I'll never be one of your warrior women." She slapped the weapon against his chest, forcing him to catch it.

"Our women are not warriors, and I'm not asking that of you. I'm asking you to take it and be prepared to defend yourself." He laid the hilt in her palm and wrapped his hand around hers.

"If something happens, you can save me," she said, her voice quavering at first, then as she continued, she gained confidence. "You're good at it. And really, if I learn to defend myself, then you'd be out of a job. We can't have that."

He smiled briefly, but this was a serious matter, one she needed to understand. "I can't always be by your side. Just because I am the only one allowed to take from you, doesn't mean others will respect the law. Since we haven't had a human here in a long time, it's possible someone will make the attempt. People break the law ever day, which is why I continue to train Guardians."

Turning the knife in her hand, she studied the craftsmanship. Or possibly contemplated her options. She glanced at him. "This is important to you, isn't it? Training them, I mean. You act like you're on a mission every time you pick up your sword."

"I am. Many years ago, my father was shot and killed protecting Lord Navarre." Soren stared at the wall across the room. He could still see it happening when he spoke of that day.

"I'm sorry."

"Don't be. He was a good man who served our lord and city well. Unfortunately my father had to die for me to understand the importance of the Guardians. Around the time it happened, I'd been skipping my training sessions. After he was killed I worked harder than any other. When I became a Guardian, the first thing I did was change the way we had been taught to fight." He leaned forward, resting his elbows on his knees.

"So you grew up," she said softly.

"I didn't have a choice. Nothing else was left for me." Not wanting her to see the pain in his eyes, he focused on the floor.

It didn't matter. If she hadn't seen his sorrow, then she'd heard it in his voice. She settled a hand reassuringly on his forearm, an unfamiliar comfort, and one he didn't know what to do with.

Her touch was a pleasant distraction. Now, instead of the memories clamoring to reach him, he thought only of her fingers wrapped around his wrist. He'd all but claimed her before his students, and after she'd admired his body in front of his Guardians, he'd practically burst with pride. This woman did strange things to his guarded emotions, had sent them all over the map in only two nights.

This whole situation was dangerous. She was dangerous.

He stood, and her hand fell away from him. "I need to check on Steffen."

Hands at his sides, he fought the urge to reach out and take her hand. She was not his mate, not his partner and confidant in life. No one spoke about his father. Not he, certainly, and Navarre wouldn't consider drudging up their painful past, but talking with her had come naturally.

He ducked out the door, and she hustled after him. Afraid of what else he might say, he kept his mouth shut tight. The farther away they journeyed from the training center, the more nervous she became. It was in the way she gripped the knife hilt, how her gaze darted here and there as the corridor darkened.

Gilded trim and colorful wall hangings gave way to bare, cold stone. The corridor became narrow and the light dim. Their path ended abruptly, a looming doorway their only option. The first step glowed a pale gray, but the rest disappeared into blackness. They needed to go one level lower to reach Steffen.

Before he hit the second step, Faith grabbed his elbow and tugged gently. The look in her widened eyes begged him to hear her. "Please don't leave me. You're going too fast."

Soren took a deep breath. He'd already forgotten the home he'd grown up in might be foreign and frightening to her. He took her hand and pulled her close, helped her down the narrow, steep, and oddly curved stairway.

At the bottom, another hall appeared, just as bare and cold as the one they'd left. Stopping at the first battered old door, he knocked loudly. No reply came, and he opened the door and pulled Faith in behind him.

"Steffen?" he called out to the darkened room.

The only answer was a man's deep, shaky breathing.

"I'm turning on a light," he warned before throwing a switch and casting a soft glow through the room.

Steffen sat on the floor, his back wedged in a corner, staring with bloodshot eyes at him through tangled hair hanging over the tip of his nose. He trembled, his hands clasped together as if they might hold his body together.

"It's not as easy as you think." Steffen's voice, like his breath, sounded hollow.

"I know, Steffen," he said, crouching near him.

"You don't." His friend's shaky whisper filled the room and he closed his eyes, a tear falling down his cheek. "I fight every night to see the next. I don't know why."

"You live to serve Navarre. You live to find your true mate. Don't leave this world and doom her to your same fate, Steffen. Be strong for her." He took hold of Steffen's head, needing to gain his attention.

Steffen finally looked at him, tears rimming his eyes. "So close. I was so close to peace tonight."

"I wish you'd stop working the gate, my friend. It's too much of a temptation."

Steffen's eyes grew wide, fearful, and looked focused for the first time since they'd entered his home. "Take me from the gate and I truly have nothing."

"Okay. Calm down. You can keep your gate," he said, soothing his fears. Steffen didn't want to die, but he couldn't help him. Steffen had to help himself first.

Soren stood, pulling Steffen to his feet and guiding him toward his bed. When his friend's head rested on the pillow at last, nothing changed. The tension hadn't left his body, and he still clasped Soren's hand as if it had become his only anchor.

Faith hadn't moved far from the doorway, and he couldn't blame her for her curiosity. She would remember Steffen, his calm confidence, the teasing light in his eyes. It didn't seem fair for her to see the same man now lying broken in his bed.

Steffen finally drifted to sleep, and he ushered Faith out the door, closing it behind them.

"Will he be all right?" she asked, and her concern seemed genuine.

"I don't know. He's getting worse. He comes home each dawn, but one day he won't return."

"Why?"

"We live a long life, Faith," he said, starting up the stairs. "Without a mate to share it with, or a purpose to drive us on, we can't ignore the call of the sun."

"Does the sun ever call to you?" Her question echoed off the walls of the stairway.

Soren paused, and for a moment, he thought he would answer her. Instead, he took her hand and kept climbing the stairs. How could he admit that he hadn't fed for nearly a year because he couldn't trust himself to face the temptation of the sun? She wouldn't want to hear that since the moment he'd touched her, thoughts of the sun and the peace it promised had vanished.

Chapter 8

———

BALINESE

"Are you finished?" Soren asked through the bathroom door for the third time.

"Keep your shirt on. You're how old? You should know what to expect from a woman by now." Faith lifted the frothy peach gown, searching for a way in. "What is this, a prom dress?"

"A what?" he asked.

"A prom..." Vampires probably didn't have a Senior Prom. "Never mind. Why is this dinner formal?"

"We dine with the lord of the city."

"That'll do it," she agreed.

She stepped into the dress, tugged the zipper up her back then caught sight of herself in the mirror, and laughed. She thought she had it under control, but she laughed again.

"What's so funny?" Soren asked, sounding closer to the door than he'd been a moment ago.

"If I had blond hair and a super skinny body, I'd look like Peaches & Cream Barbie." She'd barely gotten the words out before she doubled over, giggling hard enough, tears gathered in her eyes.

"Who?"

"I can't stop laughing." Her words came out choppy, fit in between giggles. "Don't be mad at me for not wearing this. I can't do it. The dress too ridiculous."

Putting on that peach horror would make her both fit in and stand out, but for all the wrong reasons.

"Faith, we're going to be late," he said, farther from the door this time.

She should tell him she could finish getting ready in literally ten minutes, but then, she liked the idea of him pacing and stewing. She pulled on black slacks and a gray sweater with a straight neckline from shoulder to shoulder. Twisting her hair, she pinned it, letting the ends fall loosely at the top.

She dug through the satin pockets of her suitcase for her jewelry, but instead fished out her cellphone. Holding her breath, she stared at the thing like it might bite her. She glanced at the door, then flipped the phone open. Nothing. No messages. No missed calls, and as she'd expected, no signal. She stuffed the thing into the pocket and grabbed her earrings.

Carrying the peach monstrosity, she slipped from the bathroom. "Did you really think I'd wear this thing?"

"This is the gown Elin left you?" One fist covering his mouth, he coughed, a poor attempt at hiding his amusement.

She tossed the dress at him, hitting him right in the face. Of coarse, with so much fabric, she couldn't miss. He appeared from under the gown, and draped it neatly over a chair.

"It was nice of her to let me borrow it, but it didn't fit," she said, popping on her fat little gold hoop earrings.

"It didn't fit? Did you forget I heard you laughing through the door?"

"The gown is hideous." She pointed first at the dress, then at him. "But you're going to tell her it didn't fit or else you'll hurt her feelings. Now, how do I look?"

He stared at her with such intensity from across the room, not saying a word, and her smile faltered. Perhaps her choice of a sweater and slacks would offend a vampire society.

"I can change," she offered.

Soren took a step toward her, then another. He was a breath away, and before she could speak, he'd cradled her face in his hands. She hadn't expected this, but she didn't push him away.

Eyes closed, she savored the warmth of his rough hands. Whatever had tripped his trigger brought his lips inches from hers. They hadn't made contact, but she anticipated his kiss, melting against him.

A solid knock at the door severed the moment, but not entirely. She opened her eyes as he took a deep breath, then his hands fell away from her. Behind him, the door creaked open, followed by a discreet cough. Soren regained his self-control and turned, facing the intruder.

A tall man with ridiculously long black hair loomed in the doorway like it belonged to him. He eyed them both expectantly.

"Lord Navarre, this is Faith." Soren stepped aside.

"Welcome, Faith." He gave her a slight bow. "I only stopped by to make certain you both would be joining us for dinner."

"We were leaving," Soren said.

"Oh, were you?" Navarre asked in a disbelieving tone.

Faith avoided eye contact, already feeling a prickly heat wash over her face.

"Walk with me," Navarre said, already on his way.

Soren took her by the elbow and guided her out the door. Navarre gestured as he pointed out various tapestries and artwork along the way. A light shone in his eyes as he spoke about his city. Gifts from lords of the past, treasures sent from Spain.

Faith had trouble paying attention. Soren's fingers brushed against her arm, and each stroke conjured up the image of his lips close to hers. At least, she assumed he'd planned on giving her a kiss. It would certainly have dampened the mood if she'd been expecting warm lips, and instead his sharp teeth pierced her neck.

She glanced over at Soren, who dutifully followed Navarre's gestures. How did you kiss someone with fangs?

"Here we are. Beautiful, isn't it?" Navarre asked, though he clearly expected no response.

She gasped as she entered the dining hall. Beautiful was an understatement. Sweeping red curtains bordered in gold fringe framed every doorway. Long tables formed a large rectangle in the center of the room, the outer sides lined with black chairs cushioned in red. Golden candelabras ran down the center of the tables, pinning the pristine white tablecloth in place.

The chandeliers hung low, the golden dragons on them seeming to climb out from under white glass lotus flowers. Impressively detailed, the black and gold fish scale pattern on the ceiling surrounded the chandelier, its center a delicately designed high dome. The grandeur would befit the home of any king.

A man in a powdered wig and long blue coat, complete with gold piping and buttons, played a grand piano in the corner. A light, happy song, which somehow wove the illusion of a small and comfortable room.

"Come, sit at my table," Lord Navarre offered, and they followed him, advancing slowly through the gathered people.

Vampires mingled in small groups, their low conversations hushing only briefly to observe their lord and his guests. Though she did her best not to gawk, she couldn't take herself out of tourist mode.

Women were in elegant gowns, and men had dressed in their finest. Their styles varied drastically. Lord Navarre wore black slacks with a white collared shirt, and many copied him. Other men chose to be more extravagant, wearing ruffled cravats and velvety crimson jackets trimmed in gold. A few women could have stepped off a Paris runway, while another handful seemed stuck in the eighteenth century.

Navarre cleared his throat, and Faith redirected her attention to the conversation beside her.

"Any promising young men this season?" Navarre asked.

"I'm giving you two."

"Two?" Navarre repeated.

"Yes. Titus and Dyre have skill and great instincts. Better yet, they work exceptionally well together," Soren said, holding her hand and keeping her at his side.

"Good, very good." Navarre nodded. "Though I'm not relishing the inevitable visits from the parents of failed students, especially the aristocrats."

"Nor I. They attempt swaying my decision before bringing the issue to you," Soren said.

"Soren," a young man called from the left.

His fluid stride seemed completely dangerous, feral, and it alarmed her. His approach didn't faze Soren, and that was a comfort. He stopped a few feet from them, and as he did, she noted that he stood a few inches taller than her. His lack of towering height did nothing to silence the tiny voice inside her head shouting out a warning. This man was dangerous.

"Is this her?" He nodded in her direction, his words more of a prompt than a question.

"Faith, I'd like you to meet Captain Savard," Soren said.

With what Soren put his students through, she found it hard to believe this man could best any of them, let alone lead them. How could this man be captain? He barely looked old enough to shave, and he lacked the thick muscles the Guardians possessed.

"You're the captain? But you're so young," she blurted out.

"What I do is not about age. I know the location of each of my men at any given moment. I know how many people are in this city, in this room, and who is a potential enemy. I know who is armed and who is not." The captain leaned an inch or two closer and said in a quieter version of his very smooth and controlled voice, "I know that you've been gifted with a knife. Yet you chose not to bring it tonight. You must feel extremely safe among us."

"How did you know I have a knife?"

"I didn't know, I assumed. But I know now," the captain said with a very tight, impersonal smile.

"Soren told you, didn't he?" she guessed, sending Soren an accusatory glance.

"No, I said nothing." He shook his head.

"Really, how did you know?" she asked the captain.

"It's my job." The captain tipped his head in a short bow. "It was a pleasure meeting you, Faith."

"Why did you want to meet me?" She was having a difficult time figuring out this captain.

"A woman named Faith Calburn has access to this city. A name does me no good without a face." He gave her a small, controlled smile then excused himself.

She watched him walk away, just as puzzled and alarmed as when he'd first approached. "What do you suppose he meant?"

"You'll get used to Savard," Lord Navarre said, sharing a quick glance with Soren.

"And don't let looks deceive you. The good captain is older than I am by at least a full century," Soren said.

Her jaw dropped at the hint of his lifespan. She would have liked a better explanation, but before she could ask, he ushered her to her seat. Bracketed by Soren and Navarre, she felt insignificant and completely out of place between the two powerful men.

A solid-looking woman with her hair pinned up in a tight knot made her way down the table with a cart full of plates. She set a plate before Lord Navarre, then served Faith. The smell of roasted meat made her mouth water. She took the lace edged napkin from under the silverware, and placed it over her lap as she inspected her plate.

Normal food! Thank God. "Are those mashed potatoes?"

"Mashed the hell out of 'em myself," the woman said with a wink.

"Oh, I just love you." Faith smiled brilliantly at the woman, then hunted down her fork.

"Finally, someone who appreciates me," the woman said, catching Soren in an accusing glare.

"I do appreciate you, Nelly," he defended himself.

"Aye, but when was the last time you said it?"

"Probably the last time you made me strawberry pie. How long has that been?" His eyes twinkled with playful mischief and a sweet smile curved his mouth.

"Nigh on a decade," she said with absolute certainty.

"Has it really been that long? Why would you stop making it? You know it's my favorite."

"You were getting soggy around the middle," Nelly said with a curt nod as she shuffled away.

"Proof of my appreciation," he called after her.

Faith cleared her throat to catch Soren's attention, a smile pinched between her lips. "So, you were...what did she say? Soggy?"

"When you live as long as we do, you're bound to have good years and bad years," he said, his defense somewhat playful.

"How many of these *years*, good and bad, have you had?" Curiosity tormented her.

"A couple hundred." Soren brought the wine glass to his lips, drinking deeply.

"Two hundred years old, and you still can't drive?" Faith stared at him. "On the upside, you look great."

At the sound of a few coughs and cleared throats, Faith looked past Navarre. Several men attempted to disguise their laughter.

"Thank you," Soren mumbled.

"Thank you?" A well-groomed man leaned forward and inserted himself into their conversation from the other side of Lord Navarre, his wavy black hair pulled together at the base of his neck. "All you can say is *thank you*? How on earth did you catch such a beautiful creature? You certainly didn't lure her with your charm."

"Julian," he warned.

"Really, man. We live in France. At least pretend to have an ounce of romance in your blood," Julian urged.

"Back off," Soren said, pinning Julian with a dark look.

Faith turned to Soren. "He's right, you know. We are in France. How is it that you don't have much of an accent?"

"Living underground, we don't pick up the local accents. We have a dialect unique to our city." He leaned in, dropped his voice to a whisper. "The only vampires with a French accent are those who live above most of their life, like Gustav."

"Oh," she said quietly, then focused on her food and kept her mouth shut. Apparently Gustav was a controversial subject.

Faith enjoyed learning about their strange, secluded culture, but sadly the meal ended sooner than she'd hoped. The plates had been taken away long ago, and those remaining gathered in small groups around the room. She'd half expected the men to wander off for cigars and brandy, and maybe some had, but most stayed and gossiped worse than women.

Being human, she'd assumed she would be at the bottom of the social ladder, since technically she was their food source. Instead of being scorned and rebuffed, they openly invited her to participate in conversations and treated as a guest.

Navarre bombarded her with questions, ranging anywhere from current public transportation, to vampire lore in America. Not only did he ask, he hung on every word, drinking in the knowledge she gave him.

Soren left her with Navarre, and she didn't think it strange, not until he took Julian aside. Their conversation appeared rather serious by the way they tipped their heads toward each other and spoke quietly.

"I hear your kind worship rabbits," Navarre said.

"Rabbits are nice," she said. Was Soren whispering to Julian about his Guardians, Steffen, or demons? He glanced at her, then quickly away. Were they talking about her?

"Faith?" Navarre called her name loudly.

She jumped, startled and embarrassed. "I'm sorry, I wasn't paying attention."

"Clearly." His certainty came with a quirked eyebrow. "I lost you the moment Soren walked away. Shall we join them?"

"Please." She took the arm he offered, allowing him to lead.

With each step, the better she heard them. The topic eluded her, until she heard her name.

"I'm making a mess of this with Faith," Soren said to Julian. "I'm not a social man, never have been."

"Problem being?" Julian asked.

"I haven't done a damn thing right."

"What?" he asked, then shrugged. "She's fine."

"She's here because I screwed up. She ran because I left her with Bareth and he scared her. Julian, I like her."

"Ah, I see..." Julian spotted her a few steps away and instantly shifted his demeanor. He greeted her with a cheerful smile. "We were just talking about you."

She looked between the two, suspicious. Poor Soren had that classic deer-in-the-headlights look plastered across his face. "Should I be afraid?"

"No, but Soren should be. He asked if my wife, Yasmin, would take you shopping. She would be thrilled to drag you through every shop in the city," he said, sending his version of a sly wink at Soren.

She got the distinct impression Soren had asked for help, though this might not be what he'd intended. If he wasn't going to confess the truth, she'd bite. "You have shops here?"

"Many, and Yasmin would love your company. She'd also love seeing you spend Soren's money like a madwoman," Julian said with a grin.

"I'll do my best."

A short burst of laughter came from two small children, who raced through the dining hall. The boy ran, the smile across his face positively impish as he glanced back to the little girl following him. The girl giggled, her round cheeks high and constant smiling, dark curls bouncing with each step.

The boy looked up and skidded to a halt, barely avoiding a crash with Navarre. He reached out, caught the girl before she made the same mistake. With wide eyes, both children looked past the imposing lord, their fearful gazes resting on Julian instead.

"Run, Ivette!" the boy yelled, and instantly she obeyed. He sent them a quick, bright smile, then followed her.

"Julian, were those your children?" Navarre asked.

"I do believe so. If you would excuse me, please. It's time for a chase." Julian rolled up his sleeves and dashed after them.

Several minutes later Julian walked by the doorway with a giggling child under each arm. The love they shared as a family warmed her heart. She understood why Soren adored his home and protected these people so fiercely.

"Will I meet your wife, too?" she asked Navarre, looking forward to the prospect of female companionship with Julian's wife, not to mention shopping.

"I'm afraid not," Navarre smiled sadly, gave them a short nod, and walked away.

"What did I say?" she asked.

"Navarre hasn't mated."

"I'm so sorry. I didn't mean to hurt him." Faith remembered Steffen, and as she did, concern creased her brow. "He won't, you know, be like Steffen?"

"No. Navarre won't walk into the sun. His people mean too much to him. Honestly, I believe they are what keeps him alive."

She watched with Soren as Navarre made his way around the room, talking at least briefly with everyone present. "Is he looking for his mate?"

"Are you offering to be a candidate?" he asked, one eyebrow rising.

"Absolutely not. I only meant that if he knows what he wants, he should make an effort."

"We should go," he said, turning to leave. She looped her arm around his without being asked, and he looked completely surprised. "It's not that easy for us. Having a mate is not a simple church ceremony. It's a lifelong commitment. No outs. Our legends say the only pull greater than the sun is the love of your true mate."

"How beautiful," she said, followed by a wistful sigh.

"And sad. We lose many of our kind to sheer loneliness." He dropped his head slightly.

Several chairs and loveseats lined the foyer outside the dining hall, each similarly framed by ornately carved wood. Funny, but not one of them seemed suitable for actual sitting. People lingered here, and many more trickled into hallways.

She clung to Soren's arm as he cut a path through them. One man studied her from his seat ahead. His hair shifted against his shoulders as he turned his head, followed her intently with his gaze. Before she could consider being outraged, Soren pulled her close and literally growled at the man.

Hoping to gain Soren's attention, she cleared her throat delicately. It didn't work. On her second attempt, she grabbed his hand and wrapped his arm around her shoulders. He glanced down at her, and she started walking. He could either stay by her side, or let go and get into a fight.

He kept his arm around her. Conflict averted, and point still made.

"Why are they looking at me like that?" she asked.

"They're unmated." He'd said the last word like it left a fowl taste in his mouth. Head ducked, he spoke softly against her ear. "And they know you're human."

"They want..." she began, but she couldn't focus on how to form her words as his lips moved deliciously over her ear.

"Your blood." His blunt clarification was a cold splash of reality.

"You only feed from humans?" She eyed the next two men they passed warily, feeling like live bait in a tiger cage.

"No, but you're a rarity here, a delicacy. I have no illusions they would be kind if they took from you. That's why I gave you the knife." He shifted his hand from her shoulder and covered her neck, shielding her from any lingering stares. His hand rested there intimately, possessively.

Faith smiled. For some reason, she found his jealousy extremely flattering. She didn't care for the thought of anyone else taking blood from her, but with Soren by her side, she didn't fear for her safety. With his thumb, he gently stroked her neck, soothing her. She enjoyed his comforting touch, and maybe it was even something she needed.

Tonight had not been the first time she'd met vampires of the opposite sex. "No one looked at me like that last night in the training center."

A muscle move din his jaw, and he looked away from her, then answered, "A bare throat publicly announces you want the man you're with, and that once you get home, he'll be taking your vein."

"Okay." Wow, that was a newsflash. "If the neck thing screams that I'm into you, then why are they not getting the hint?"

"Because we're not mated," he whispered. "If I were not by your side, you'd be giving them an open invitation."

She smacked him square in the chest. "Why did you let me leave your home with my hair up?"

Soren stopped, faced her, and slid his hand down her arm to take hold of her hand. "I needed every man in the dining hall to think you want only me and to believe I'm taking your vein tonight. Vampires are often respectful when they see mutual desire. I used your ignorance to help keep you safe." He tipped his head slightly as he studied her. "You held your head high and carried yourself like you were born to this life. Having knowledge of the gesture would have made you self-conscious."

"I was self-conscious. I didn't fit in." Without the customary ball gown, her confidence had taken a nosedive, but Soren had easily built it back up.

"You did," he said, not sounding pleased, put his arm around her shoulders, and headed home.

Each step left the dining room and bustling corridors farther behind. Now they were alone, and the silence here seemed strange. More so as a man approached, his boots hitting the stones with a heavy, even stride. His downcast face and sweeping hair barely hid his burn-scarred face.

"Osric," Soren acknowledged him.

The man gave no response, and Soren didn't elaborate. The short exchange reminded her that she was here to stay.

They arrived at his home, and the steady support of his hand fell away from her neck as he closed the door. She heard him lock the door soundly, and stepped away from him and into the bedroom, where she kicked off her heels one by one.

"I'm exhausted." She stretched from side to side, then searched for the pins in her hair. "How long do you think it will be before I adjust to your reversed days and nights?"

"Not long," he said, suddenly behind her.

The heat of his body enveloped her from shoulders to hips, and she nearly jumped as his hands settled on her arms.

Her stomach fluttered with anticipation. She wanted his hands on her, his arms around her, but he hadn't budged. Maybe he waited for her response.

She leaned back, and he required no more encouragement. Head dropped, he hovered with his lips over her shoulder. She shivered, his heated breath skating across her skin. Soren kissed her there, the warm pressure penetrating her thin sweater. Then he slowly, sweetly, moved inch by delicious inch, but didn't stop at the base of her neck. He kissed his way higher, until his lips played below her ear.

"Are you going to take my..." She couldn't bring herself to say the word 'blood', and as he pinched her earlobe between his lips, lost the word entirely.

"I'll take anything you're willing to give me." His deep voice sent uncontrollable shivers through her, and she chased them with a soft sigh. He made every female bone in her body yearn to let him truly have anything.

Then, with tenderness, he nipped at her neck. Her eyes snapped open, a sharp awareness cutting viciously through her bliss. He had no emotional ties to her. She was being used. He wanted the blood she could give him. Nothing more.

She pulled away from him, tense and still, no longer pliant. Too many other males had eyed her neck tonight, craving the same thing as Soren.

Unable to look him in the eye, she ducked away, taking long steps until she reached the bathroom, then she locked the door behind her. She needed to think, or maybe to forget how the bottom dropped out of her stomach whenever he held her.

She clung to the hope of forgetfulness. After all, she'd completely overlooked his species, until his teeth had grazed her neck.

She turned on the faucet and drew a bath. The steam swirling above the water promised a less complicated kind of comfort. She'd soak, and relax until her fingers wrinkled and the tension left her muscles.

It worked too well, and she woke much later, surrounded by tepid water, the scent of lavender thick in the air. She stepped out of the tub, making a point to avoid the clock. After slipping on her pajamas, she left the bathroom and tiptoed to bed.

An odd noise broke through the room, stopping her in her tracks. She held her breath, waiting. The noise came again, soft and rumbling. It almost sounded like snoring. She followed the sound, and found Soren sleeping in the chair he'd slept in the night before.

She hadn't escaped him as she'd soaked in the secluded tub. Soren drew her in with his kindness and consideration, captured her with his touch. He'd become a permanent fixture in her mind and memories. He could have hurt her or taken what he wanted, and yet he hadn't. Maybe he didn't want anything from her, didn't want *her*. Anyone could provide blood for him, but the idea of him wanting only her blood was hard to swallow.

She tiptoed closer and stood between his outstretched legs. He didn't move. A small nightlight gave the room an orange glow, the light playing across his face. She reached out, touched his cheek. The rough shadow of whiskers scraped her fingertips. She brushed her fingers through his dark hair. He felt like a regular man, and yet was something else entirely.

"You don't have to wait until I sleep to touch me," he said, eyes still closed.

With a yelp, she retreated backwards until the bed hit her legs, forcing her knees to buckle. Luckily she landed on the mattress, though without an ounce of grace.

"Go ahead, do what you want. I promise not to move a muscle." He smiled wickedly.

She pulled her feet off the floor and plunged them between the covers, turned her back to him.

"No? Perhaps some other time," he teased, without opening his eyes.

Chapter 9

———

BALINESE

Soren hurried home, hoping to get there before Faith woke. Thursdays were always a mixture of lies, exhaustion, and time management. He'd lived like this for over a year now, as had Elin. The doctor's daughter, a petite beauty, was his midday Thursday appointment.

Long after the Guardians left the chateau above, abandoning it to the sun's rays, they would meet in the spacious ballroom. Thick curtains clung to the windows, blocking out daylight.

He'd never tell a soul about their private meetings, and neither would she. If anyone discovered Elin took lessons in the art of combat, it would be disastrous. No repercussions would fall on him for teaching her, but for a female, fighting of any sort was social suicide. Friends would reject her. Males wouldn't consider her for a mate. Her family might disown her.

Elin understood the consequences, and still wanted to learn. Each Thursday they battled, and she continued to surprised him with her commitment and skill. She was improving.

He was late again, and would have enough time to rinse off his perspiration in the shower, throw on a change of clothes and run out the door. He relied on Faith to keep her promise and remain here, and it felt entirely odd. However, she could not be trusted with his secret concerning Elin. Faith would be awake by now, and if she asked where he'd been, he would have to lie for the sake of Elin's safety.

He rushed into his home, slammed the door behind him. Wide eyed, Faith hopped out of his way as he barreled through then marched straight into the bathroom. He needed to get in and out fast to avoid an incriminating conversation.

The shower flipped on, and for a moment, Faith stared at the door. Hadn't he already showered for the night?

A few minutes later the water stopped running and the bathroom door unlatched, opening a crack, but Soren didn't come out. She peeked in. He had a towel wrapped around his hips, and standing before the mirror, ruffled his fingers through his wet hair. Sure, she'd seen a few half naked men up close in her lifetime, but none of them had physically worked for a living. Soren did, and it showed.

He caught her glazed stare in the mirror and grinned. Busted.

Soren sent her a playful wink, then turned back to the mirror. "Your breakfast should be here in a few minutes."

He'd done it on purpose. He didn't need to know how much his bare flesh affected her. Her attraction to him last night had unsettled her, even more so after she'd factored in his vampire genealogy. Today seemed to be headed in a similar direction.

A knock came at the door, thankfully. She opened it, and a man hurried in and set a small tray on the coffee table. After giving her a short bow, he left.

Beneath the tray's lid were all sorts of fruits and fruit-filled pastries. She'd just popped a whole strawberry in her mouth, when Soren came from the bathroom. The earthy, herbal smell of his soap wafted through the room.

There was something reassuring in the way he moved with such purpose. A busy and important man here, he carried himself with a quiet confidence. Soren tucked his shirt in quickly, then walked to the wall and hefted a large battleaxe from its perch.

"You're not going to use that on those boys, are you?" she asked, horrified.

"Damn straight, I am. And they're lucky it'll be me they face instead of someone who means to kill them with it," he said, resting the thing over his shoulder.

"You have a point. But would your enemies really use an axe?"

He shrugged, surveying the tray of food. "Not that I'm aware of, but I refuse to let them be ignorant."

He snatched a blueberry muffin and headed for the door.

"Wait for me," she said, running after him.

"Today you're staying here. Yasmin will be by soon to take you shopping. Get anything you want."

"But I..."

"I mean it, Faith. Anything you want. Buy a whole new wardrobe. Redecorate my home, if it makes you happy."

"Are you sure?" What man in his right mind would give a woman carte blanche to redecorate his entire house? Especially when many items here must have belonged to his parents. She'd feel odd removing anything that was his, but an addition or two couldn't hurt.

"I trust you. But if you take down the weapons, wait until I return."

"Because they were your father's?" she asked, finding it hard to believe he would allow anyone to move them.

"They were, but I don't want you getting hurt with one. They're old, heavy, and I keep them sharpened," he said, and waited expectantly for her agreement.

"Got it. No playing with the crossbows and broadswords." She gave him a thumbs up.

"Good girl," he said, readjusting the battleaxe over his shoulder. "I'll be back after last meal."

"Okay."

He'd walked out the door, when with a sudden urge to make him smile overcame her, and she ran to the door and called out his name. Halfway down the hall, he turned toward her.

"Can I at least wear the Viking helmet?" she asked.

A grin broke across his face. His eyes sparkled. "Absolutely."

She closed the door, pleased that she'd pushed away the itch to be shy. When he smiled and she was the cause, her stomach did funny flip-flops. Plus, he'd been sweet enough to send her shopping.

Now she faced an outing with a woman she'd never met. A vampire. She was nervous, but women being women, a common ground was always shopping, right? She rummaged through her suitcase in search of shopping clothes, a concept only a woman would understand.

Pulling on her nicest underwear and socks, she quickly made the switch. Slip-on-shoes were a must. She had no intentions of tying laces or zipping boots all day. Lastly, she pulled on a shirt with a wide collar.

The wider the collar, the less the hair got mussed. She looked at herself in the mirror, smoothing the dark red shirt over her hips.

A knock sounded at the door and she swung it open. In the doorway stood a perfectly poised and beautiful woman. Her long black hair curled in thick waves with half of them piled on top of her head, giving her the look of a sultry Roman goddess.

"Hi, I'm Yasmin," the woman greeted her. "Julian said your name is Faith. Did he get it right?"

"Yes."

"Bravo for him. I was certain he hadn't paid attention again." She smiled, one of those secret smiles married women seemed to have when gossiping about the men in their lives. "Ready to make Soren regretful?"

"I would be, but he left in such a hurry and didn't give me any money. I'm so sorry. I guess I'm window-shopping today."

"Oh, you've a lot to learn, my dear. The shops in Balinese are nothing like your stores above. All you have to do, is drop Soren's name and they'll send him the bill. You'll have a ton of sway in the shops since you're attached to a powerful man." Yasmin turned from the doorway, leading the way.

"Oh, no. We're not actually attached," Faith corrected, walking beside her.

"Really?" Yasmin gave her a disbelieving look. "Can I ask you a question?"

"Sure."

"Have you ever been told what you are, what your position is here in our world?" she asked gently.

"He said I belonged to him." She held her breath. What had he kept from her?

"You are his, but what you are is a servant. His servant. We don't like to use the word slave, but in essence, that is what you are," she said in a quiet tone. "It has nothing to do with you personally, it is simply the unavoidable role of a human in our world."

That bastard! Being stuck here and being Soren's personal blood donor was one thing, but a slave? "I don't know what to say. I want to scream, cry, and then take one of those damn weapons off his wall and chop him in half."

"Don't be angry with him, Faith," Yasmin said, patient and motherly.

"I am angry."

"Let me tell you something honestly. Julian told me he's never seen a vampire male show genuine care and concern for a human. Soren is the only exception." Yasmin took her arm, pulled her to a stop. "Faith, he treats you as if you were his mate, his wife."

"No, he doesn't."

"Servants wear drab brown clothing, yet you are allowed your own. Today he sent you shopping, with an aristocrat, no less. You sat between Soren and Lord Navarre in the dining hall, but servants are not permitted to attend unless they're serving food. I also heard Soren defended you against some powerful council members. Julian didn't say in what way, but he said the display made it evident to everyone present that he cares for you a great deal." Yasmin patted her arm and continued walking, and patiently let her digest this information. "My point, Faith, is that he treats you as his mate because he wants you for his mate."

"He said I was his the other day, but I thought he was being protective or egotistical." A lump had risen in her throat. Perhaps he'd only been protecting his property.

"Tell me exactly what he said." Her eyes brightened at the prospect of girly gossip.

She chewed on her bottom lip for a moment. How exactly had the event unfolded? Oh, yes. "One of the men meant to toss me out of the training center. Soren stopped him, threw him to the ground, and gave him a serious lecture on touching another man's woman. He had a short temper with those boys after that."

Yasmin clapped several times, beaming. "I'm right. I knew it. He's hooked on you."

"I don't think so. Soren's seems a good man, a gentleman. Perhaps it's in his nature to protect, and he would take care of someone weaker than himself, which I am by two counts. Female and human." What Yasmin had said made sense, but was not completely convincing. Soren had been good to her, true, but she wouldn't mistake kindness and consideration for affection. Especially if she was just a servant in his world.

"Perhaps, but do open your eyes to the possibility," Yasmin said, ushering Faith into an elevator.

After a moment, the elevator doors opened to the next floor lower, and Faith hesitated. On the level Soren lived on, everything was calm, orderly, and decorated in a wealthy fashion. Here the corridors bustled with people, and although the same flat gray stone covered the floors, unique designs separated the doorways of each shop. An entirely different world.

This corridor stretched on, an underground mall filled with people hopping from shop to shop. Faith couldn't stop staring at each door they passed. One shop looked like someone's home, complete with a couple curved steps leading to the door. Another had a glass storefront with a rotating door in the center.

Her favorite had been the store for children's attire. The front brickwork was painted brightly, and the top half of the door left wide open, but the bottom half remained shut. The clever little gate penned the rambunctious children.

Yasmin rubbed her hands together. "What are we looking for?"

"I have no idea. I'm having fun just being here," she said as she turned around to watch a woman pass by with hundreds of braids twisted through her hair. "Soren said to get anything I want."

"He didn't," Yasmin said, a look of complete amazement on her face.

"He practically demanded it."

"Then you simply must have anything you want." Yasmin paused, a finger on her chin. "Julian said you didn't wear a dress to dinner the other night. We should start with the necessities."

"I'd rather not. I'm not much of a dress kind of girl." She shook her head, images of the peach gown returning to haunt her.

"Maybe not, but certain events such as dining with the lord of the city requires proper attire. At least two would make a good start." Yasmin eagerly pulled her into a shop with crystal teardrops swaying in the narrow windows.

Yasmin went straight for the racks, but Faith held back. This was awkward. First, she didn't like frilly things. Second, she didn't have the height to pull off most of these gowns. It was depressing, but Yasmin refused to let her sulk. Like a professional shopper, she displayed one after another for her inspection.

Faith turned down a frothy and feminine pink gown, and a sleek black with a neckline that dropped down to her bellybutton. Not in a million years would she touch either one of those.

However, they did find an intriguing green dress with a beaded hemline, and Yasmin persuaded her to buy a red satin gown that showed off a great deal of her back. The idea of wearing a gown held such romance, but she'd never been the type. Her practicality demanded she cling to her blue jeans.

"Which one will you wear tonight?" Yasmin still shifted the hangers left and right, making sure she hadn't missed a great find.

"Tonight? Why, what's tonight?"

"Soren didn't tell you? Tonight two of his students become Guardians. It's a grand and private ceremony. Students who do not advance won't even be aware of what's happening tonight," she said, relinquishing the hunt.

"Now they can swing their swords around like barbarians, right?" Faith asked, lifting her gowns onto the counter.

"You've got it." Yasmin laughed.

"Then the red one seems appropriate," she said with a smirk.

"Hello Yasmin," the clerk behind the counter greeted Yasmin with a warm smile. "Will these be on Julian's account?"

"Yes, these three. The other two?" Yasmin elbowed her, prompting her to speak up.

"Soren's account, please," she said, guilt already creeping in over the expensive purchase.

"The red will be perfect." Yasmin looked past her, and her smile faded.

A tall, slender woman brought up a dress and placed it onto the long counter beside Faith. Following Yasmin's hesitant gaze, she was shocked to see a woman inspecting her closely.

"You must be Soren's new toy I've heard so much about," the woman said, displeasure dripping from her voice, her sleek hair motionless as she turned her head toward her.

"Excuse me?" she sputtered out the words. Who just says something like that out loud? She was no one's toy!

"He's only playing with you, human. He won't keep you," she said with a nasty smile.

If this woman wanted to play dirty, so could she. With a sugary smile, she placed her hand on the expensive dress. "That's for Soren to decide, not you. At the moment, I'm being kept, and rather well I might add."

"We're running out of time, Faith. Soren will simply kill me if I don't have you back by five for the ceremony, and we have more shopping to do." Yasmin hooked her arm through hers and steered her out the narrow door.

Once they cleared the doors, Faith grumbled, "Miss Priss was one more smart remark away from a black eye."

"You're serious, aren't you?"

"I'd like to punch her just to see her perfect hair get knocked out of place," she fumed. "Who was she, anyway? One of his old girlfriends?"

"I don't think so, but I could be wrong," Yasmin said. "You need to understand that vampire women dream of being mated to a Guardian."

"But you aren't," she pointed out.

"Julian wasn't always a councilman. He'd served as a Guardian first." Yasmin laughed and gave her a small shove. "Don't look at me like that. I know I'm as bad as the rest of them. It's difficult to stop chasing a Guardian once you've been close to one."

"That woman shouldn't be jealous. Soren's not a Guardian." Faith said, as if Yasmin's reasoning didn't apply.

"Oh, but he is. He may not stand guard with them, but he has in the past and trains them now. Soren answers only to the lord and the captain. A man can't get any more powerful around here. It's what drove that woman to a fit of jealousy. She saw her chance at snatching wealth, peerage, and power taken away by a sweet human."

"That's what she wanted? What's wrong with having the man?"

"I knew I'd like you. Come on, I've got a surprise." Yasmin urged her toward a different elevator.

She followed Yasmin into the elevator and down another floor. The doors split open, and the difference here was huge. The stores had rougher exteriors, and though still beautiful, didn't have the same kind of class as those one floor above.

The first store on her right looked odd enough that she stopped to figure it out. Larger than the others, it had a double facing of white brick, which led her to believe it was one large shop. The design, however threw her a curveball. It had three different entry doors. "Am I missing something? Is it separated inside?"

Yasmin sighed wistfully. "Ah, Cyprian. He's brilliant. The only reason you'll ever see an aristocrat on this level is because of him. Each door brings you to the same open area. The trick to finding what you're searching for, or so he says, is to enter through the door that suits you best."

"Well now we have to try it," she said, catching her bottom lip between her teeth as she studied the doors.

The first door was wooden, arched at the top with two panels of beveled glass, simple and gothic. The second rested on two round brick steps. Made of darker wood, a dozen thin squares of glass filled the door. The third had two long panels of stained glass depicting tree branches covered in bright green leaves and scattered with vibrantly colored birds.

Yasmin went for the birds, while Faith opened the second with its overload of glass panels. The appeal hadn't been the door itself, but the urge to climb the brick steps.

The other side was one large room filled wall to wall with furniture and unique decorations. Beneath a hanging of swallows in flight stood a triangular shaped chair. The couch beside it was fluidly carved and upholstered in diamond white. The coffee table had been carved into a life size tortoise. These pieces were genius, brought to life by an amazing artist.

"When Julian and I were married, we bought everything from Cyprian," Yasmin said, clearly lost in happy memories. "I suppose you're not looking for furnishings, though."

"No, but I think his home is missing something," she said, scanning the room.

"Soren is missing something?"

"There." She pointed to a table one aisle over. This was precisely what she wanted. "He doesn't have a chessboard. This will fit right in with all the weaponry."

"Go on and have it sent to him. I haven't shown you the surprise yet and we're running out of time," Yasmin urged.

Faith took the chessboard to the cashier, and smiled all the way out the door, pleased she'd found something for Soren. As she left, although it made her feel silly, she just had to exit by the same door through which she'd entered.

Yasmin's big surprise was paradise. A short walk later she was in the midst of stores selling jeans, sweaters, T-shirts, and all the cozy pajamas a girl could desire. She hadn't seen a fancy gown here, not one sequin or bead.

The people here had transformed shopping. The true icing on the cake...her arms weren't loaded down with bags or boxes, and the bills would be delivered to Soren's home, along with everything she'd bought. A brilliant system, but the convenience made it hard to know when to stop.

Exhausted, and finally finished shopping, she sat with Yasmin in a café. The smooth, rich chocolate pie paled in comparison to the piping hot hazelnut coffee they leisurely sipped. The sidewalk beneath her feet in this underground café had cracked with wear over the years. If she didn't know better, she would think she sat at a Paris café in the evening. Dark walls faded out of sight due to the streetlamps shining bright onto the tables, and above them, tiny stars dotted the ceiling.

"Can I ask you something about Soren?" Faith asked.

"Sure, anything," Yasmin said, wrapping her hands around her cup.

"I haven't met his family. Is that because of what I am?"

"No, dear. He doesn't have any family," Yasmin said kindly.

"Everyone has family, even if it's the crazy uncle no one talks about."

Yasmin shook her head. "Not that I'm aware of. Soren's mother didn't live long enough to give him a sibling."

"He said his father had been shot protecting Navarre."

"Soren and Navarre are roughly the same age, and when they were younger, neither took their places in life seriously." Yasmin stared at her coffee. "An assassin killed Navarre's father. When he went after Navarre, Soren was with him. Soren's father was shot while protecting Navarre, and the assassin escaped."

"How could he escape? The Guardians didn't stop him? The captain? Soren wouldn't have let the man get away."

"It was over before anyone knew what had happened. Soren was young then, untrained and in shock. Things changed after the assassination. He worked harder than anyone I've ever known to become a Guardian. Once Navarre accepted him, he gave Soren free reign over his Guardians. Sometimes I think he trusts Soren more than his own captain."

"He still has Navarre," Faith said, setting aside her empty coffee cup. "He's not family, but at least Soren still has his friend with him."

"They're still friends," Yasmin said, nodding slowly. "But Navarre is much more stoic than he once was, and is more lord than friend. That night changed Navarre, too."

She sat quietly for a moment, letting everything sink in. "I had no idea he was alone."

"He's not alone." Yasmin reached across the table to squeeze her hand, then caught sight of her watch. "Oh! We've got to go. The night is ending and we need to get ready for the ceremony."

Hurrying, she followed Yasmin, who headed off in a different direction from where they'd come. Dozens of feet down the busy corridor, a sharp right, and they walked straight into an elevator.

"I don't know how you do it," Faith said, leaning against the elevator rail. "This place has too many twists and elevators. I'd be lost in five minutes."

"It's easy. If you're ever lost, you can hop into an elevator, press one, and wander around until something is familiar. I'll show you," Yasmin said with a nod.

The doors slid open to the first floor, but nothing was recognizable.

"These are homes." Yasmin pointed to the handful of doors scattered spaciously throughout the long hallway. "In fact..."

Yasmin walked up to a door, knocked loudly, then grabbed Faith's elbow and sped down the hall several feet before turning back. Julian stepped out, a bowtie twisted in a knotted mess to the side of his neck and barrettes snapped randomly in his hair. Several long strands had been knocked loose, hanging at odd angles.

Faith covered her mouth to hide her smile, but Yasmin let her laughter roll loudly through the hall.

"You think this is funny?" Julian asked. "Ivette is getting me ready for the ceremony. I talked her out of ribbons, but apparently pink bow barrettes are in a completely different category."

"You look beautiful, dear," Yasmin said, as if appeasing a child.

"I need help. Are you coming back soon?" he asked, glancing over his shoulder into his home.

"I love it when I get to save the day for once," Yasmin said with a sly smile, then turned to her. "If you take a left at the end of the hall, you'll pass the dining room. Can you manage your way home from there?"

"Better than he can handle being dolled up." She nodded to Julian, who still waited impatiently in the doorway. "I'll see you both later."

Faith gave them both a quick wave and headed toward Soren's home. This was the first time she'd really been alone. It felt strange, even though being alone wasn't an unfamiliar sensation. After her parents would begin their nightly round of arguments, she would disappear to the back yard, hide among the thick evergreens. She'd been alone then, and after her parents had split.

They'd fought over her, but never for her. Living with her mother had been like being haunted by a ghost. Faith knew her mother lived with her, knew where her room was located, but she'd rarely caught sight of her. Moving out had been a surprisingly peaceful type of solitary life.

At work, however, she'd been surrounded by oodles of people, but no one wanted to make friends with the boss's daughter, and she hardly blamed them. It hadn't been that he gave her special treatment. In her father's eyes, she was another worker bee—easily dispensable, easily replaceable.

All in all, she was an expert at flying solo. So when Yasmin had appeared pleased to bustle through every store time allowed them, and answered any question she thought of, it had thrown her. The notion of having a friend was foreign, but what else could Yasmin now be?

And Soren? Outside of her childhood home, she hadn't lived with anyone. For the most part, he'd been considerate and sweet. Something she hadn't expected from her constant companion. And definitely not a vampire. She smiled a secret little smile. He was growing on her.

Following a sudden impulse, she made her way in the general direction of the training room. She found it easily. Either she had a great sense of direction, or she'd been lucky.

Peeking in the open door, she kept still, not wanting to disturb the class. Soren stood in the center of the room with a group of young boys in a full circle around him.

"Tell me why, Gian," he said, and she held her breath, his deep, smooth voice sending a funny tickle to her stomach.

"Fists aren't weapons. You can't defend yourself with them," a young boy with long black hair answered. Her last visit here, he'd been one of the more coordinated youths.

"Step back boys. Gian, take the sword," Soren said, passing him the weapon. "Now attack me."

"I can't attack you, you're unarmed." Gian grasped the hilt even as he eyed Soren in disbelief.

"Then it should be a short fight." Soren's rough, confident voice filled the room.

Gian lifted his sword and came at him with decent enough skill, but Soren easily dodged the blade, gripped the boy's shoulder, and planted him face down on the floor. A grunt came from Gian. His sword had been knocked free of his hands.

"Well done, Gian." Soren pulled him to his feet.

"It didn't feel well done," Gian mumbled, obviously stunned by his speedy defeat.

"Your body is the most powerful weapon you have, and sometimes the only weapon." Soren walked the inner circle now, looking each boy in the eye. "You won't always be armed, and you shouldn't have a sword when you feed. You cannot panic your prey or give humans a reason to take issue with you. Guardian or not, you will not be armed if you walk off this property. Learn the strengths and weaknesses of your body, and you'll live longer."

The boys looked between each other, uncertainty in their expressions.

"You still don't believe me?" Soren challenged. "Answer me, Dario."

"You can do more damage with a sword," the boy with darker, exotic skin answered.

"You want to do damage? Do you know what the deadliest creature alive is?"

"That's easy. It's a demon," Dario said with a cocky shrug.

"Right, but do you know why?"

"They're stronger," said one boy.

"They're bigger," came from another.

"No. It's because they have no conscience, no heart. Those creatures would bleed out a child, given the chance. Demons rarely carry weapons. They don't need them. In all my years, in all the battles I've fought and all the gruesome things I've seen, the weapon that did the most damage were the teeth of a demon." Soren gripped Dario's shoulder. "Damage is not something to strive for, Dario. If you do, you're no better than a demon."

The boys stood motionless, eyes wide and fixed on Soren. Clearly this was not the lesson they'd anticipated learning.

She hadn't expected his answer either. Suddenly craving the safety of Soren's home, she backed away from the doorway. If demons could tear a throat apart like a wild jungle cat, then her escape from the demons in Paris would never have happened, if not for Soren.

As dangerous as demons were, Soren had defeated three with his bare hands. A shiver raced up her spine.

She practically fell through the door to his home, shutting it behind her hastily. She needed a distraction, a task to keep her mind busy and away from visions of bloody teeth. Thankfully a small mountain of packages awaited her, piled neatly beside the coffee table.

Chapter 10

———

BALINESE

Faith's adjustment to the reverse day and night schedule hadn't been as difficult for her as Soren might have guessed. At least, he'd assumed it hadn't until he'd come home to find her collapsed in his chair. He sat on his haunches, shaking his head at the sight before him. Her dark, disheveled hair fell over her closed eyes and down her neck. Bare feet planted firmly on the cushion, she curled her knees against her body, supporting both her head and her left arm. She was sound asleep.

He gently lifted her free hand and traced her fingers. In sleep, with her breathing deep and even, she didn't flinch or shy away from his touch. Too bad it couldn't be like this when she was awake.

Last night as she'd retreated into the bathroom, her sole purpose to avoid him, he couldn't mistake her reaction for anything other than fear. Had she dreaded their connection, or the creature he was?

Those fleeting moments before she'd bolted had been a small start at gaining her trust. True, her arms had remained at her sides, and she'd made no move to touch him, but she'd allowed the heated contact.

For years, he'd avoided intimacy and relationships in any form. They'd left him empty, and he'd moved on without an ounce of regret. Since he'd met Faith, the ground beneath him had shifted. Everything pulled his thoughts to her. Tonight he'd left the training center early and hurried home, because she would be waiting. He'd opened the door, and had been instantly hit by the scent of her perfume. Faith was home.

He craved a lifetime with this woman. An impossible conclusion in her human state. He had to be careful. Faith was still unsure of her surroundings, including him. If he pushed too hard, she might retreat further away from him. They had plenty of time together, and if he remained patient, perhaps she would come to him.

He turned her hand over, drew soft circles on her palm. The large, sweeping motions brought no reaction from her, but as the spiral shrank and closed in on the center of her palm, her fingers twitched. He smiled.

Her eyes snapped open, and she pivoted in the chair, kicked out and slammed her feet hard against his chest. Unprepared for the assault, he was pushed away far enough she was able to lock her knees and hold him at bay. Eyes wide open and wild, she glared at him through rumpled hair. Beautiful.

"Calm down, it's just me," he said, laughing softly.

She pulled her bare feet off his chest as if he'd scalded her, then dropped them onto the floor. "You scared me."

"I only meant to wake you. I'm sorry, but if I let you sleep we'd be late for the Induction Ceremony." He stood and gave her space, backing away from the chair. "We've got an hour before we need to arrive at the main hall. I hope you bought a dress you're willing to wear."

"I did, and an hour is plenty of time." She shoved herself over the deep arms and off the chair. "We won't be late."

He pressed his lips together at the sight of her bolting away yet again. A frequent occurrence he intended to fix.

His suit lay spread out across the bed, and since she'd safely barricaded herself behind the bathroom door, he took the opportunity and changed. While wrestling on his shoes, a small pile of empty boxes piqued his curiosity. He scanned the room and found the receipts from her shopping trip.

One by one, he studied the slips of paper, a frown settling in place.

"Faith?" he called.

She popped the door open and peeked out, makeup on and hair mostly curled. "What?"

He held the bills, and as the stack of slips in his hand caught her eye, she cringed.

"I'm sorry it ended up being so much money. Yasmin kept throwing things on the counters. I told her to stop, but her idea of *anything I want* was completely different than mine."

He took a couple steps closer. "I have only six bills. We have over a hundred shops in this city. Why didn't you buy more?"

"More?"

"I have a feeling Yasmin's ideas were the same as mine. I meant what I said." He took a breath, giving himself a short moment to think. Why had she only bought a few things? Maybe stores were different above, or money. "Faith, I have the means to provide for you. Let me."

"I didn't want anything else. Honest," she said, still hidden behind the door.

"I find that hard to believe." He dropped his hand, the papers crinkling together as they hit his leg.

"I'm fine. If I think of something I need, I'll buy it. I promise." She laughed, a lovely joyful sound, and shook her head at him, then wrapped a chunk of her hair around the curling iron.

He would fight her on the matter. Haul her back to the shops and bring home anything her eyes settled on.

Then the door drifted open wider. He managed to raise an eyebrow, but did nothing further. Frozen in place, he devoured the sight of her in a black satin robe. The thin wrap tied at her waist and left her legs bare from mid-thigh down.

She cleared her throat, and he had the good sense to make eye contact, but it didn't last long. He caught a quick glimpse of her mirthful smile. She must have expected him to say something, but what had they been talking about?

"Did you get that today?"

"I did," she said, tugging the belt a touch tighter.

"I'll make you a deal. Buy two more of those, in different colors, and I won't make you go shopping again tomorrow." He'd heard his words, hardly believed he'd said them, and his gaze once again returned to her legs.

"Deal," she said, and as she turned, the slit in the side of her robe presented him with an extra three inches of bare thigh.

"Good Lord above, I'm going to die a slow and pleasurable death," he mumbled as she eased the door shut. "How did he die? Oh, you know that woman he brought home? Yeah, that's how it happened. Did she murder him? Nope, just wore a tiny robe around the house. Heart gave out."

She giggled, then said loud and clear through the door, "You'll live."

Soren stared at the wood paneled door. She'd heard him. Great. Now he had nothing to do but sit, wait, and ponder the acoustic nightmare that was his home.

A short handful of minutes later, Faith emerged. Large, sweeping curls hung loose around her shoulders, scattered with tiny curled braids. The brilliant red satin gown shimmered in the light.

The word *elegant* came to the forefront, along with a few others in the same category, but then she turned away from him, plucking her earrings from the dresser, and those words slipped off his tongue at the sight of her exposed back. The gown resumed coverage below her rib cage.

"That's the gown you bought?"

She spun slowly, displaying the gown and smiling. "You like it?"

"Depends on who looks at you." He shrugged the black jacket over his shoulders. "I should have hired you a guard for the night."

"But I thought..."

"I prefer you in jeans." His clipped words mirrored his sudden sour mood, and before he sabotaged himself further, he took her elbow and led her from the room.

She was completely his when she wore jeans, the way he'd found her, and he missed them. Now she wore red satin, the thin fabric slipping sensuously over her skin as she kept pace beside him.

Her damned gown caught his gaze with each step she took, the fabric skimming over her thighs like a lover's hand. Being a gentleman was becoming less desirable by the minute, especially when pulling her into the nearest room and ravishing her had been the only thought knocking around in his head since they'd left home. Thankfully, the main hall was just ahead.

Before they reached the room, Faith stopped and pulled her arm from his. She stepped back and faced him, fists clenched tight at her sides.

"What's wrong with the dress?" she demanded, every bit a statue as she awaited his answer.

"Nothing. It's not your dress," he admitted.

"Then you have a problem with me." She'd lowered her voice, but spoke with certainty. "Yasmin mentioned I'm a slave."

He closed his eyes and drew in a long breath, then opened them. "You're not a slave. Humans are either executed or they're servants, that's the way of it."

Truthfully, he'd assumed she'd never know if he didn't tell her. The label his people placed on a human was irrelevant.

"So I'm a servant?" Her eyes flared wide, then she whispered harshly, "As in, pour your wine and bring you your slippers?"

"Technically speaking."

"I'll tell you exactly where you can put your damn slippers." She gave him a glare and spun away from him.

This was his fault. He'd made her doubt herself because he'd neglected to tell her the truth. He blocked her path, catching her in his arms.

"You're not a slave or servant, Faith. Not to me. Not ever." Lingering with his lips against her temple, he kissed her there and whispered softly, "My mistake forced me to bring you into my world. I regret taking you from all that is familiar to you, your home and family. I'll always owe you a debt I cannot repay."

He'd been certain she teetered on the verge of crying, either from his words, or the loss of her family. Instead, she reached out, ignoring the slight gathering of tears in her eyes, and brushed her thumb across his chin.

"You should have told me."

"Another regret." She was right. He'd piled them high lately.

"If you don't have a problem with the dress, or with me, then what?" Head tipped back, she looked up at him, concern creasing her lovely eyebrows. "I don't like not knowing where I stand with you."

Soren shook his head slightly, surprising himself when he answered, "I'm not handling this well."

"Handling what?"

"Jealousy."

"You're jealous?" She blinked several times, paused, expectant.

"I will be. We're walking into a room full of Guardians, a majority of whom are unmated. I'll be put to the test at some point." He glared at the door.

She lifted her chin, squared her shoulders, and snatched a pen off the guest book table. Elbows in the air, she twisted her mass of curls onto her head, and jabbed the pen through the center.

With her messy, sexy hair piled high, leaving only a few random curls flying out of order, she took his arm.

She'd done it again. Just when he'd gained control, she'd gone and done something which kicked his heartbeat up a notch.

"What are you doing?" He'd basically breathed the words.

"Making a statement. I'm here with you." She smiled up at him, sweet and inviting.

If she needed to make a statement, then by heavens, he'd let her. He steered her through a set of tall, golden double doors, pride bursting in his chest. She was claiming him.

Under their feet, a narrow white and gold carpet ran from the doors to the opposite side of the room, climbed two steps and ended at the base of an overly large chair.

"I thought you said this was the main hall. It looks like a throne room." Faith held tight to his arm, studying a column which sprouted from the green marble floor where it melted into the domed ceiling above.

"Officially it is, or was. The lord's decision is still supreme and final, but we rarely use this room now that we have a council," he said, guiding her along the edge of the room.

Yasmin waved, drawing their attention over the crowd. Julian stood near the front, a hand low on his wife's back, completely comfortable in the midst of their aristocratic peers.

"Another good year, I expect," Julian said, stepping aside and making room. "Navarre said you made a surprising choice. Can't wait to see what you did this time."

"I think I was more surprised than him." Soren smiled politely, but despite his best efforts, couldn't seem to attend to the conversation. He'd released Faith's arm, intending to give her a bit of freedom, but she hadn't let go. Standing at his side, biting her lip as she scanned the room, she held his hand. Willingly.

"Soren," Captain Savard called, giving Faith a glance before halting in front of him. "Is it true?"

He nodded, restraining a smile at having ruffled the captain's cool reserve.

"Let's get it over with." The captain squared his shoulders, then mumbled under his breath, "Damn. It's hard enough to babysit one."

"Yasmin, take good care of her," Soren instructed, and promptly followed Captain Savard.

The ceremony began almost immediately after Soren left her side. Captain Savard stood at Lord Navarre's right, and Soren at his left. The crowd had split. Each half stood to the sides beneath the columns, waiting eagerly for the ceremony to begin. Yasmin had said over a hundred guests would be present tonight, and her estimate appeared accurate.

The elegant double doors opened, and Faith turned to see with everyone else as two imposing warriors strode to their lord. The hushed murmurs swirling around the room didn't distract them, gazes fixed on their destination. As the men came to a halt before Lord Navarre, they bent to one knee, planted their fists firmly on the step.

In unison, their voices rang loudly through the hall. "I wish to serve my city, with my life and with my blood."

"Who gives these men to the service of Balinese?" Lord Navarre asked.

Four people separated from the crowd, clearly the boys' parents, and replied, "We do."

"Who proclaims these men prepared to serve Balinese?" This time, Navarre's voice was not as loud.

"I, Soren Rayner, proclaim these men ready to serve." He then gave both of them a sword.

Each man grasped his sword tightly, holding the hilt chest level, blade up. The blade was not flat against their face, but perpendicular, allowing them to look upon their lord.

The urge to applaud almost made her give in, but everyone around her stayed silent.

Together the two men said, "I swear to serve my city, with my life and with my blood."

"Then do so. I accept you both. Rise, my Guardians." Navarre gestured to the crowd.

They stood and turned, blades still raised, showing no emotion. Every man and woman in the hall clapped wildly, and she happily joined in as they moved past her, their swords still before their faces.

Once the new Guardians had left, the crowds on both sides of the room came together in a crush, talking and raving about the ceremony. Some bantered with each other over who had known the new Guardians the longest. Fame through association.

Flexing her fingers at her sides, Faith chased away the tingling sensation from clapping, and couldn't stop smiling. She'd seen the work Soren had put in with them, known how hard those men must have struggled to get to this point in their lives. She was proud of all three men.

Soren shook hands with several men as he pushed his way through the churning crowd and headed in her direction. He caught her watching him, and smiled. She responded with an instant and unfading smile. Cutting conversations short, he kept moving until he stood before her.

"You shouldn't disappoint them. They want to talk to you." She looked behind him to the clusters of men nodding and chattering in a lively manner, and occasionally pointing in his direction.

"Then they can come to me. I didn't want to leave you alone." He practically grinned from ear to ear. "What did you think?"

"It was quick, and strange, like a marriage ceremony." Parents had given them away, and they had each been given symbols of their new rank.

"I supposed it is a marriage of sorts," he said, tilting his head to the side as he thought it through. "They bound themselves to the city, swearing to protect it with their lives. It might be a quick ceremony, but it's a life long and life changing commitment."

"How often are Guardians accepted?"

"Not as often as you might think. On average, only one is accepted in three years. Occasionally we'll take one per year, but that's rare. This is the first time I've ever given Captain Savard two at once. He's not pleased, but he doesn't know them yet. He'll change his mind." His short, confident nod would have convinced anyone. Soren pointed the new Guardians out in the crowd. Swords now sheathed at their sides, they received congratulations from their families and noblemen of the city. "Do you remember them?"

To her, that particular group had been a blur of fighting men. In their exhausted state, they blended together in her memory. Not to mention, Soren was the one who had her full attention. "I think so. I remember they stuck together."

Soren nodded. "That they do. I've never met two men who were such opposites and yet such good friends. Somehow they're always tuned in to what the other is thinking."

"What are their names?"

"Titus and Dyre. Titus has the short hair, Dyre the long." Proudly Soren watched them, his chest puffed.

"You look forward to the moment you get to see them make their vow to their lord. This is what you work for every day, isn't it?" she asked, though she saw the answer on his face.

"It is." He wrapped his arm around her and hugged her to his side. She stilled, though not wary of him or uncomfortable. Sharing this achievement with him made her a part of him.

Several men and women came and congratulated Soren. Some teased him, saying the new Guardians had better be damn good since he'd passed two at once. Soren had no doubts, and that seemed to placate them. Faith hadn't said a word to those who approached them, and no one spoke to her. Her lack of conversational participation left her free to observe.

A man stood in the middle of the crowd, staring her down, his harsh, ice blue gaze shaded by lowered eyebrows. Shivering, she broke eye contact. The urge to run surged, but instead, she breathed even and deep to calm the unreasonable desire. He must have someone else in his sights because she'd never met him.

She glanced at him once more. He now marched toward them, and she remained the focus of his sharp gaze.

She tugged on Soren's sleeve until she caught his attention, then whispered, "Who's that man? He was staring at me, and now he's coming at us."

Soren zeroed in on the man approaching them and pulled her behind his bulky frame. From here, she couldn't see a darn thing.

"Is that her?" the man asked, his rigid voice growing ever closer.

Staying in the shelter of Soren's body, she peeked around his shoulder. Something dark and angry bubbled under the surface of this man, and he scared her. She squeezed Soren's hand and put her trust in him.

"Yes," Soren said slowly. Head dropped slightly, he tightened his hand around hers, and studied every move the man made.

Her breath caught. Soren had this kind of focus when he fought. Oh, God. No!

"She might be remaining in our city, but this is not the place for a servant," the stranger said, top lip curled as he swept her from head to toe with his gaze.

Soren stepped forward, but Navarre gracefully placed himself between the men and addressed the hawk-eyed man.

"Vidor, my friend," Navarre cautioned. "She is Soren's guest. In fact, I think she is the loveliest addition tonight. Now, gentleman, I will remove the object of your disagreement."

Navarre reached around Soren, took her hand, and pulled her away from the feuding men. When she glanced back at Soren, he stood with clenched jaw, watching her go, helpless to argue against his lord.

Not exactly a delight for her either. No one would bother her at Navarre's side, but since he'd whisked her away from Soren, she had a nagging sense of being exposed. Vulnerable.

"I'd rather stay with Soren. Please." She twisted her hand to free herself from his grasp. The attempt failed.

"Now is not a good time. Let those two stare daggers at each other without you in their crossfire. Trust me when I say that spending a few minutes with me will put to rest any question of whether or not you are accepted among us." His grip loosened and Faith nodded, letting him guide her across the room. The crowd parted for them, or more accurately, for Lord Navarre.

"Would you like something to drink?" he offered eagerly.

Soren seemed miles away on the other side of the room, too far away for comfort. "I need a drink."

Navarre let out a short laugh, then handed her a goblet. She took it and swallowed the limited contents in a few good gulps. The alcohol burned for a second, then warmed her belly.

"Don't let Vidor shake your confidence," Navarre urged.

"You're the one practically encouraging them to fight it out." She shook her finger at him. "Why not just tell him to back off?"

"It's not that easy. Vidor helped my father build this city. It's been hard for him to see many of the laws he wrote altered or abolished." Navarre ducked his head, releasing his breath in a huff. "He needs confrontation, and not only from me. The more who oppose him and force him away from the past, the better he will be able to cope with what our lives are today."

"Why does it have to be Soren?"

"My dear, you are the root of their disagreement." He paused, then said low, "This isn't the first time they've had words over your presence in our city. Soren defended you then, and I believe he always will."

When she searched for Soren in the crowd and found him, he stood alone and aggravated. Her first instinct screamed to go soothe him, but being the topic of his recent argument, would she be welcome?

He scanned the crowd, and when he'd found her, the worried crease on his brow lessened. They were connected, had been since the alleyway above. She couldn't pinpoint the moment he'd become vital to her, but she understood the subtle pull between them. She missed him. He was right in front of her and she itched to get closer.

The orchestra startled her as they struck up their first song of the evening, a peppy, unfamiliar tune.

"Would you like to dance?" Navarre asked.

"Oh, I don't think I will." She gave up. He'd already pulled her to the center of the floor.

Navarre expertly spun with her, weaving around other dancers, and gliding across the marble floor, she followed his lead. Her feet struggled to keep up with him, and she stumbled several times. With each bobble, heat scorched her face. A simple dance shouldn't be embarrassing. Navarre didn't seem to notice her distress and carried on, comfortable in his skin. Over and over he compensated for her mistakes.

Their dance ended abruptly as Bareth stepped into their path. This time when confronted by his intimidating size, she planted her feet, refusing to shrink away.

"I'm cutting in. You're going to need this," Bareth said, handing her a glass of wine and motioning for her to drink.

Faith sipped deeply, then lifted her eyebrows delicately. "How did you know?"

Bareth snatched the glass with a grin on his face. Shoving the half empty glass into Navarre's hand, he then took hold of her hand spun her around the room. The warm wine buzzed inside her head and threaded through her muscles, loosening tension.

Regardless of Bareth's complete lack of grace, she had more confidence with him as her partner, largely due to the fact that they weren't actually dancing. The man flung her around like a rag doll.

"You don't have daughters, do you?" she asked, catching her balance.

"Yes," he said with a nod, then shook his head. "Well, not exactly."

How did that qualify as an answer? "You'd better explain."

"I have a son. Gretta's pregnant with our second. For her sake, I hope it's a girl," Bareth said, grinning from ear to ear.

"Congratulations. But boy or girl, promise me something?" She gripped his arm when he made yet another harrowing turn.

"What's that?"

"Let your wife teach the children to dance." Eyes closed, she battled a wave of nausea.

"What's wrong with my dancing?"

"I'm getting dizzy," she admitted.

Bareth's laugh was plotting, unapologetic, and without a doubt the most nerve wracking thing she had ever heard.

In the blink of an eye, he sent her spinning away from him. With nothing to hold on to, her balance failed, but instead of landing flat on her face, she crashed against a solid wall of a man. He instantly wrapped his arms around her and she tensed, ready to yell for help, but it was Soren looking down at her, and she couldn't help but smile.

"There you are, my protector." She leaned forward, rested her head on his shoulder. "Want to dance?"

"No," he said stiffly. "I don't dance."

"Thank God." She took a deep breath, grasped his arms for support. "Don't let him spin me anymore."

"Never again," he said as if it were an absolute fact. "Should we head home then?"

"Not yet. I think I'm still spinning." She squeezed her eyes shut and melted against him, relying on him to keep her standing.

She felt him shift as he tried to get a better look at her face. "How much did you drink? Our wine is strong."

"Now you tell me." She sighed into his shirt.

"Are you going to be sick?"

"Maybe. What's wrong with him? Why would he spin me so much?" She lifted her head, took a deep breath, then patted his shoulder. "I'll be fine."

He skimmed his thumb over her cheek, slid it down and stroked the edge of her bottom lip. "I've got you."

"I know. That's what I love about you," she said, leaning into his gentle touch.

Their gazes locked. He'd heard the shocking word *love* slip past her lips. Her heart pounded furiously. What would he say?

For that matter, how would she respond? Just because she loved something about him, didn't mean she loved him. But the word had a life of its own, and it hung between them.

Waiting for his reaction was like teetering on the edge of a cliff. Her gaze dropped to his lips, and as it did, the warmth of his hand settled on her exposed back. Flesh on flesh tumbled her barriers and jacked up her heart rate. She bunched the fabric of his shirt in her fist, dragged him closer.

Soren's hand engulfed her shoulder, then he slid it to her wrist, untangled her hand from his shirt. Tense and wary, she held her breath. Was he pushing her away?

"Not here," he whispered, then a blast of cool air separated them as he stepped back.

He clasped her hand, and before she could sort out what had happened, they were headed out the door. Laughing, she raced along with him.

Chapter 11

———

BALINESE

Faith stirred, consciousness slowly returning. She had no interest in waking up. If she did, she'd only brood over what went wrong. They'd come home at a brisk pace and she'd had ever intention of ending up, well, with him, right where she lay now. Three steps in, she'd tripped over the stupid gown. Not her most graceful moment.

She'd changed quickly, emerged from the bathroom and discovered herself to be alone. What had gone wrong? He'd had her. She was a sure thing, and he'd walked out. Disappointed and confused, she'd climbed under the covers to keep warm, certain he would return soon. Somewhere between then and now, she'd fallen asleep.

A groan escaped her. It was too late to avoid that emotional ride. She'd just relived the whole day, or was it night? Morning? Oh, whatever.

She opened her eyes slightly. Soren's chair was parked several feet from the bed, abandoned. She didn't know the time, or how long he'd been gone. Eyes shut against the large, empty chair, she rolled over, burrowing under the covers until they brushed her chin.

A soft snore broke through the rustling blankets. She stopped moving and listened intently. Had he come back? Maybe he had, but the sound seemed different, misplaced.

He snored again, this time louder and closer. Her eyes snapped open and she stared at him, stunned. Soren lay stretched on his back beside her. Sometime in the night he must have joined her under the covers.

She flipped onto her back. He couldn't sleep in a chair forever, she understood that, but a warning would have been nice.

His silhouette was just visible. Only his chest moved, his breathing deep and even. Above that mesmerizing rhythm, the shadow of his whisker-dusted jaw. Soren had a habit of being clean-shaven and ready to face the day. She hardly got a chance to catch him like this, all rough and rugged.

What if he didn't shave tonight? On second thought, it might be a bad idea. The temptation of skimming her sensitive palm over those course whiskers would be too great. She'd already caved once.

The desire to put her hands on him had been present and screaming at her since she'd watched him spar, bare-chested, with the Guardians.

She flopped onto her side, facing away from him and once again confronting the empty chair. She very much needed to redirect both her mind and body.

Her efforts might have worked, but the weight of Soren's thick arm curled around her middle and he dragged her to him. His chest pressed against her back, his muscled thighs warmed the backs of her legs. Unprepared for the full contact of his body against her spine, she flinched.

"You move too much," he mumbled, his words slurred by sleep.

His heat seeped into her, and little by little, she relaxed in his embrace. Content in the tender cradle of his powerful arms, she sighed. She'd needed this from him.

He'd become comfortable to her, familiar in this strange world. Safe. She slipped her hand in his. Within minutes, she'd matched the cadence of his breathing, and the steady rise and fall of his chest lulled her ever closer to sleep.

Then he burrowed his face against her neck. She gasped, shoved her hand between her neck and his face. Would he bite her? Hurt her? He could, easily. From his lesson to the youngest class, if a demon's teeth could damage skin horribly and painfully, then by sound logic, so could a vampire's.

Soren moved behind her, lifted his head. She squeezed her eyes shut. Her heartbeat thumped in her ears.

"I am not the animal you think I am. I will not drink you dry in the night." His harsh whisper in her ear sent a volley of shuddering chills spreading over her arms and down her legs.

She'd upset him, but it couldn't be helped. The man sported a set of fangs. She had ignored the facts as much as possible. After all, he possessed several wonderful qualities. He was considerate, a gentleman, and she genuinely liked him.

Being bitten again had held a certain amount of intrigue at first, but no longer. In the dark of night, when it might actually happen, fear had crept in and overwhelmed her. Soren was right. She'd assumed instinct would take over and he'd lose control.

The mere placement of her hand had cut him deeply. Pain had laced his voice and proved she'd hurt him, but she couldn't bring herself to bare her neck.

"Take your hand off your neck." His agitated demand had come out in a growl. "I won't bite you."

"I know that," she whispered, but didn't move her hand.

"Then why cover your neck?"

She swallowed her pride and told him the truth. "I don't remember what it felt like."

One long, deep breath came from him, and for several moments he said nothing.

"It's hard to describe," he said in a low half-whisper, no longer sounding as irritated. "Being human, it would probably feel different to you anyway. For the most part, it's enjoyable."

"I can't remember if it hurt, and I certainly don't remember anything being enjoyable."

"You wouldn't. The blinding pleasure we are capable of giving is like a sedative to humans," he said softly. "You only recalled my bite because adrenaline pumped through you."

"Oh." She had no idea how to respond to his unexpected answer.

Soren pressed her shoulder to the mattress until she lay on her back and he loomed above her, but he didn't crowd her. "I have no need for blood now, and unless I'm injured, I won't feed for several months. When the time comes, I promise to ask your permission."

"You will?" Then she asked tentatively, "But what if I say no?"

"I'll go to another." The statement fell lifeless, flat.

"I have your word?" she whispered. He nodded, and she wrapped her arms around him, hugged him close.

Stretched out on the mattress, he kept her tight against him, locking her there in his strong embrace. She didn't protest. In fact, she clung to him, molding herself to his side. He gave her the freedom to make a choice, and she adored him for that.

Groggy, and not exactly awake yet, Soren rubbed his face with both hands. The pillow beside him had been abandoned. Letting out a deep moan, he rolled onto his stomach, and stuffed her pillow under his. He'd missed his bed. No more kinked neck and stiff back.

The bathroom door opened and Faith stepped out. Smiling, he watched her lazily, and tilted his head to keep her in his line of sight. Her hair strayed left and right, and her cheeks were flushed.

She carefully placed her clothes in his bureau. No more suitcase on the bathroom floor. Each time she opened those drawers, he took it as a sign that she accepted being his permanent guest.

Now she folded the black robe and tried to place it in the drawer, but the slippery satin wouldn't cooperate. It simply refused to remain folded. After several attempts, she stopped, huffed out a frustrated breath, then dropped the thing in a crumpled heat inside the drawer.

His smile spread to a grin. He couldn't stop the snowball effect, and his grin morphed into an all-out laugh.

With a yelp, she shut the drawer and spun around, eyes wide. "I didn't know you were awake."

This woman had wrapped her arms around him last night, slept at his side, then she'd thanked him for a promise he would keep, if only because he wanted her willing, eager, and...

That damn turtleneck again. Her cozy cotton illusion of protection had been a barrier against him from the beginning. Did she think him the kind of man who would forget a promise overnight, a beast who took what he wanted? Fine. If she held such a low opinion of him, who was he to disappoint her?

He threw off the covers and rolled of bed. The hunter inside him had awakened, and he had a target.

"Soren? Her voice brimmed with uncertainty. She had nowhere to go, and in two backward steps, collided with the wall.

Picture frames rattled around them as he slammed his palms hard against the wall on each side of her head. Her lips parted, and a panicked gasp escaped. Head ducked, he took her lips in a searing kiss. He held nothing back, pouring his desire, yearning, and his very soul into kissing her, loving her.

Her hands touched his chest hesitantly, and he growled low in his throat, taking a step closer. She pulled away, but only for a second. Sliding her hands over his chest and around his shoulders, she kissed him back. Tugged greedily at his lips with hers, pulling him closer.

Afraid of what he would do if the slow burn she ignited got out of control, he kept his hands on the wall. He'd never shared a kiss this wild and consuming. Desperate to touch her, he curled his fingers against the wallpaper. Had he already gone too far?

She pressed herself flush against him, and he hissed, grasped her hips, fingers spread wide. The heat of her body beneath his fingertips nearly did him in, but regretfully, he collected himself enough to pull away from her.

She gripped his shoulders, struggled to bring them together again. He was able to keep their bodies apart, but unwilling to break the frenzied kiss. He had to end this, and fast.

As he slid his hands over her hips and up her rib cage, he took her shirt, moved higher with his hands. The heels of his palms grazed the sides of her breasts and she gasped for air only to take in his tormented groan.

Tearing his lips from hers, he pulled her shirt over her head, returned for one more delicious kiss, then turned on his heel and walked away.

"I'm burning this damn thing," he growled, holding up her turtleneck as he left the room. The door slammed shut behind him.

Wearing only her bra and jeans, she stood in his home, stunned. He had to put distance between them, but he'd only made it through the door. With her shirt wadded in his hand, he'd stuttered to a halt. He'd kissed her. God, how he'd kissed her, and he wanted to march right back in there and do it again.

With a curse, he strode to the nearest trash basket. The soft thump announced the turtleneck had reached the bottom.

Faith tipped backward, and her shoulders met the wall with a thump. She let the wall support her and stared at the closed door. He'd walked away. How could he kiss her with such passion then leave? Maybe it meant nothing to him, but she'd put her heart into that kiss.

After her neck had a close encounter with his teeth last night, she'd needed the false security of the turtleneck. It concealed the part of her that he desired most. At least, that's what she'd thought a moment ago. Now she wasn't sure it was her blood he favored. He hadn't touched her neck.

Shivers skittered over her skin. He'd kissed her completely, intimately, and not once had she considered his fangs as he'd devoured her lips.

The excitement inside her mellowed, and nervousness crept in, spurring her into motion. A step, then two, and she walked aimlessly around the room. She pulled her hair away from her face and up in a ponytail. Time to get serious and sort out her emotions instead of letting them run rampant. But at this point, recognizing logic would be difficult. She lived with a vampire in an underground city. The whole situation was nowhere near logical.

Did that mean her former life had made sense? No. The constant solitude of home and work had been grating on her for a while. Come to think of it, home hadn't crossed her mind until now.

She dashed to the bureau, tugged open the top drawer, and dug under her clothes. Her hand wrapped around the cool plastic cellphone. It had a low charge, and a poor signal. No messages and no missed calls. In the past she might have been angry, or even cried, but the blank screen killed what little compassion she had left for her parents.

She grabbed a random T-shirt from the open drawer, threw it over her head, stepped into the hallway, and retraced the path leading to the chateau. The first night she'd taken this same path, escape had been on her mind. Tonight was no different.

She opened the heavy door, pushed her way through. The chilled cement floor permeated her bare feet as she hurried through the cellar and up the stair. Guardians would be at the gate, but she had no plans to venture further.

Again, she checked the signal. The cell had great reception at the top of the stairs, not far from the kitchen windows. Soft beeps echoed through the kitchen until she found her dad's number. It rang several times, then his voicemail snagged the call. He never answered his phone, not even for her.

If she'd had any doubts about her intentions, they were gone now. Her parents wouldn't change, but she had.

"Hey, Dad. I found a place and a job in Paris. I'm not coming home. Tell mom for me. 'Bye." She didn't have anymore in her. Neither of them had bothered to find out where she'd disappeared to, or called to make sure she hadn't been killed. No more waiting for them to genuinely give a damn.

She marched down the stairs to Balinese, and tossed her phone into the first wastebasket she passed. The resounding clunk left a satisfied smile on her face.

Soren cared for her. She refused to throw that away because of his fangs.

Her search for him took her past this home to the end of the hallway. She found him, arms brace on the balcony railing. He stared out over the pond. Standing there in his pajama pants, he bore no resemblance to the monster his kind had been portrayed as over the years.

"Soren," she said quietly, tiptoeing toward him.

"Go back, Faith," he growled.

She stopped, tilting her head slightly. "Are you angry with me?"

"Yes, I'm angry. You think the only thing I want from you is blood." His ribs expanded with each deep breath.

Okay. Point taken. "What is it you want from me, then?"

Soren turned, pinned her feet tot he floor with the sincerity of his gaze. "Everything."

"What?" she asked, and rocked back.

"I won't lie to you. The urge to bite you beats at my skull when you're near, but not for blood. I want you in every possible way a man wants a woman." He clamped his mouth shut and turned away from her, looked over the water again. "Why were you in Paris?"

"Is it important?"

"No." He shook his head. "Just wondering why fate threw you at me. That night was the first I'd set foot in Paris in over a year."

"This may sound funny, but I'm here on my honeymoon," she said simply.

A dark scowl settled on his face. "I see. You don't seem very brokenhearted about losing your mate."

"My what?" Oh, no. He'd thought she'd been married. Recently. She quickly shook her head and clarified, "I'm not here with a man, husband or otherwise."

"Explain," he said, gaze fixed on her.

"I packed my bags and took a solo vacation. Every girl dreams of her wedding day, even the ones who claim they don't. Pairs always fits the fairytale, whether it's the wedding, honeymoon, or ten year anniversary. It's a girl thing. I just needed to get here." Admitting to her failed hopes and dreams was embarrassing. Head tipped downward to hide her face from him, she leaned against the railing beside him. "This is difficult for me, you know."

"What is, being here?" Hip on the railing, he turned to face her.

"Not really, but yes."

"Explain that, if you can," he challenged.

"This is a beautiful home, comfortable and warm. I can have anything and everything I ever wanted. I'm living with a handsome man who provides these things for me." She tried to sound practical, remain composed as if she recited a list, but as he stood taller at her side, she had to smile.

"You find me handsome?"

"I'd like to find you naked... Oh!" Hands covering her mouth, she shot him a look. Soren grinned from ear to ear, dashing all hopes that he'd missed hearing the *N* word. Her cheeks warmed, and she dropped her gaze to the pond. "Well, that's not my point."

"Too bad," he said, and when she glanced at him, the spark of desire flared between them instantly.

She had to get this off her chest, and the way he bit his bottom lib between his teeth derailed her thought process. She tapped his arm with the back of her hand.

"Stop it, Soren. My point is that none of it's mine. It's like I'm playing at being married, but this isn't my home. You don't belong to me." She paused, wistful. "I can't recall having anything that was completely mine, something I could take care of, be proud to call my own."

"You didn't have a home?"

Her brows pressed together for a moment before she answered him. "I had a home, but my dad bought it for me. My mom picked out the furniture, then paid gardeners to 'update' the lawn. Dad retaliated with buying me a car."

"Retaliated," he repeated. "How does one retaliate with a car?"

"That's how they prefer to fight with each other. I think it's a habit left over from their divorce. They lured me with gifts in the custody battle, but neither actually wanted me. Both liked to win, whether it was the house, the boat, or the kid. One day I came home and found a key and an address in an envelope on Dad's kitchen table. Dad bought me a house. He picked it out, and he owns it." She speared her fingers through her hair, angry with them all over again. "Damn it, I just want something of my own."

"You want to go pick out a cat?"

Faith laughed. He'd broken her streak of gloom. "No. Thank you, but no. I don't think I qualify to take care of something living. I had a goldfish once, and that didn't turn out well."

"Okay, no animals. I guess that rules me out."

"Soren, I don't think of you as an animal. I never have." She'd heard the pain in his voice, though he pretended it didn't matter. "I like it here, I really do, but I feel like an outsider in your life and your world. I don't know where I belong. What if I don't belong here?"

Soren pushed himself away from the railing. "Would you marry me?"

The whole sentence floated, wonderful, magical, something so enticing... But, "I still won't fit into your world. Marrying me won't fix anything."

"There's nothing to fix. I only want you," he said.

" I...I don't know," she stammered. She'd had every intention of giving their relationship a real chance, but marriage?

"Give us a chance." With his fingers he brushed through her hair, tucked stray pieces behind her ear. "It is all yours, Faith, with or without marriage. I'm yours. Whenever you're ready."

Chapter 12

―――

BALINESE

She'd expected Soren to ignore what had happened between them. Instead, she'd caught him watching her throughout last night with carnal heat in his eyes. She'd been just as bad. Every time he spoke, her gaze had drifted to his lips.

Odd tension had always popped between them, and now she easily recognized it as desire. Mutual desire. The night had already started off with a few lingering glances that had left her lost in a daydream, her cup of Earl Grey forgotten, cooling in her hands.

The bathroom door swung open and she turned her head to the subject of her fantasies. He sat on the edge of the bed, a shoe on one foot and the other in his hand. She slowly entered the bedroom and paused, pressed her shoulder against the doorway. Why would Soren be dressed completely in white?

"You're not dressed for class. Where are you going?"

"I'm teaching."

"In that?" She pointed at him from head to toe.

"The first day of practice for a new Guardian is ceremonial. Titus and Dyre will also be wearing white. We fight for first blood," he said as he stood.

"What?" She straightened, horrified and hoping she'd heard him wrong.

Soren took one look at her expression and laughed. "The intention is not to hack off limbs, Faith, only to draw blood. Rarely is anyone seriously injured."

"Sounds like fun," she said with a fake grin.

"You're welcome to stop in and watch," he offered.

"I wasn't any help last time you brought me with you. Because of me, multiple boys got lectured, and you knocked one on his ass. I think I'll stay here," Faith said with a short nod.

He put his hand over his heart. "That really hurts, you know. I thought you liked watching me practice."

"I did," she said quietly. She bit her lip to keep from smiling like a ninny.

"So, the truth comes out." He met her in the doorway, filling the small space. "You ready to marry me yet?"

She cleared her throat. "You can't expect me to marry you based on attraction."

"No, but attraction is half the battle, and it appears I've already won that," Soren said with a wink, then dashed out the door.

After the door latched shut, she wandered into the bedroom and pulled out her jeans and brand new button up black shirt. She skimmed her fingers over the collar. She'd bought it with Soren in mind. In fact, he often occupied her thoughts.

The door flew open and she gasped. Soren strode in, and she was relieved to see him. Until he advanced on her. Each step he took kicked her heartbeat up a notch, and in an instant he pinned her to the dresser, deliciously crowding her.

He leaned closer and she shut her eyes and parted her lips, ready to accept him. His lips didn't make contact. Instead, he brushed his cheek against hers, his lips moving against her ear. "I forgot my guns."

"Liar." The accusation had come out as more of an airy whisper.

He backed away, the smooth slide of metal against wood verifying his story. Smiling, he holstered the weapons and walked out.

Damn it, but the man was a tease. He hadn't kissed her on purpose. Hands planted on the dresser, she steadied herself. She'd given her one phenomenal kiss, offered marriage, and now he was holding out on her?

If he planned on tormenting her, then she'd have no remorse over doing the same to him. She might as well go watch him practice.

One cold shower and a half an hour later, she hit the training room, and was instantly puzzled by the silence. No one shouted. No swords clanked together. Titus and Dyre sat alongside the wall, speaking to each other in hushed voices.

"Where's Soren?" she asked, and both men jumped to their feet.

Titus coughed, then sent Dyre a nervous glance. How odd. Titus seemed the more boisterous of the two, but he kept quiet, his eyes avoiding her.

Dyre answered. "He's been injured."

"Where is he?"

"The medical room is three doors down on the right," Dyre said.

Faith was in motion before she could comprehend her destination. Gripping the door frame, she whipped her body around the corner and ran. Navarre and Julian lingered in the hallway. She didn't wait to reach them before she called out.

"Is Soren in there? Dyre said he was injured."

"Yes, he was," Navarre confirmed.

"Is he...does he need blood?"

Julian stepped closer, leaning forward. "Actually, he does. I was just going to call her."

"Her? Who?" she asked, clenching her fists at her sides.

"Excuse me. Julian?" Navarre interrupted, but Julian waved dismissively at his lord.

"A woman Soren used to see. She'll allow him to feed from her," Julian said, and pressed buttons on his phone.

"You put that phone away. He doesn't need her." Pushing up her sleeves, she barreled past the two men.

———————

The chilly metal table had finally soaked up some of his body heat. Soren sat on the edge, making an effort to remain still. If he turned his head, or reached for anything, pain darted throughout his back. His multiple wounds hurt, and blood still poured from them, but he smiled like a proud father.

Titus had beaten him. Okay, technically Titus had sent him crashing backward into the glass display cabinet, but blood was blood. The way Titus had rose to the challenge of First Blood had taken him by surprise. Now he sat here, bleeding and cringing, smiling. All right, maybe just a half smile. Titus was one of the finest Guardians he'd trained.

The hallway door opened, and shut quickly. Julian's satisfied laugh floated in from somewhere outside the room. Word must have traveled fast. Soren carefully turned his head to his visitor.

Wide eyed, Faith stared, a hand clamped over her mouth. Damn it, she'd seen the blood. He had no mirror to verify his condition, but he guessed that he'd lost plenty.

"Faith, I'm fine," he said gently, attempting to relieve the panic in her eyes.

Without an ounce of hesitation, she planted her hips between his legs. She gathered her dark hair in one hand, gave it a quick twist, and held it away from her neck.

"What are you doing?" he asked, leaning away slightly.

"Bite me."

Soren struggled to comprehend her short, urgent response. "What?"

"You heard what I said. Bite me. Go on, get it over with," she said, squeezing her eyes shut, teetering forward.

Would she truly allow him to drink from her? "Faith, you don't have to do this."

"Oh, shut up and do it. You need blood, and I won't let that other woman touch you. I don't want you to die," she pleaded.

"Faith, I'm not...what woman?"

"Damn you, Soren. Bite me." She took hold of his neck and brought him down to her.

The glass in his wounds sliced new paths through his flesh, making him groan. His palms caught the edge of the table, halting any further movement. He tried breathing through the pain, but it didn't help a damn thing. His expanding rib cage tugged at the freshly torn wounds. Gritting his teeth, he dropped his head to her shoulder. She curled her fingers through the hair at his nape, and the simple strokes were comforting. He seriously owed whoever had sent her in here fearing for his life. She'd offered herself, persistently, and he wouldn't turn her down.

He shifted slightly, brushed her delicate throat with his lips, nuzzled her there, stalling long enough for her to escape him should she change her mind. She only gripped his neck tighter.

Swiftly and with skilled precision, he broke through her skin. She went rigid in his arms. Her breath came in short bursts. Unlike when he'd fed from her in the alleyway in Paris, here she would remain conscious and fully aware of him.

Shivering, she dropped her hair and clung to him. She'd crossed the threshold, gone from the shock of the bite to the blissful pleasure of feeding. He took only enough to build her passions, to demonstrate that his bite wouldn't harm her.

Prying one hand off the table, he wrapped his arm around her, cradled her. Stinging pain skittered across his upper back, and a muffled grunt escaped him.

He slid his fangs free, and a muscle in his upper lip twitched. His instincts rebelled against sealing the bite. If he left the bite open to heal on its own, she would be marked as his, but he couldn't make that choice for her.

He pushed past the urge to mark her and ran his tongue over the bite. With a gasp, she pulled back and searched is face, her rosy cheeks and passion-glazed eyes a lovely sight.

"How are you?" he asked as he ducked into her line of sight.

"I'm...I...that was..." Her words gave out, and her knees. She gripped his thigh and caught herself.

He grinned. "I bet it was."

A door slammed behind them, and she jumped. Soren turned slightly to see the intruder. It was Elin. She'd come from the adjoining room with a flat tray under her arm and a fistful of medical tools, and she glared at him as if he'd just become her number one enemy.

"If you don't mind." Elin pointedly ignored him, directing her words at Faith with a fake smile plastered on her face. "I need to fix Soren."

"He's fine now. You won't be feeding him," Faith snapped.

Elin recoiled, but only for a second. "Excuse me? What kind of place do you think we run here?"

"Elin, it's okay," he said, carefully shifting so he could see her.

Elin glanced at his back, then narrowed her eyes on him. "You know I'm not a surgeon. Two minutes, Soren. You couldn't have waited two minutes? Now I'll have to slice you open and find the pieces. Next time, keep your lust contained until after I've pulled the glass from your back."

She was all brimstone and fire, but his only concern was for Faith and the betrayal in her eyes.

"Glass?" she asked Elin, and stepped out of his arms so quickly she stumbled. "You mean he wasn't dying?"

"Death by broken glass? Are you kidding me?" Elin let out a strange half snort, half laugh as the tray hit the table with the clatter of metal on metal. "Only if we're talking about slicing his head off."

"I didn't need to...to..."

"I tried to stop you," Soren said, though he hadn't. Not really.

Faith stared past him, unfocused, already blocking him out. She turned to Elin, a comrade of sorts now that they were on the same page. Mad at him. "Don't give him anything for the pain when you take out that glass."

A conspiratorial smile crossed Elin's face, and she wiggled the small scalpel between her fingers. "Hadn't planned on it."

"Good." Faith spun on her heel and rushed out the door.

"Faith, wait," he called, but she refused to turn around, and she didn't stop.

He gripped the edge of the table, intent on following her, but at the first sure touch of the scalpel, froze. He let out a howl, twisting and glaring at his tormentor.

"Hold still," she snapped, not intimidated by his bellowing. She carried on, leaving a stinging trail of short, lightning quick incisions from left to right.

"What do you expect, woman? You're carving me up. You couldn't wait until I was ready?"

"You didn't wait for me. Serves you right," she said as she added more glass to the growing, sticky pile. "I'll have to slice you open at least half a dozen more times to get all this out. You're bleeding, again. And you have one seriously angry female waiting at home. I hope that was well worth it, Soren."

"She's worth it," he amended.

"Good. Then hang on, because we're having another go at this." Elin sliced through his skin once more, quick and sharp. Soren groaned through the next handful of cuts. He caught his breath only to have his stomach turn as the sticky glass was plunked onto the metal tray.

The door popped opened, and he straightened. Had she come back? No. Navarre entered, followed by Julian, who caught sight of his back and didn't bother hiding a grimace.

"Soren, you look..." Navarre's words dropped off as he encountered the bloody mess.

"Well," Julian supplied with a smile. "You look well."

"He's sitting in a puddle of blood, boys." Elin's mousy voice softened her berating words. "Get over it."

"I don't want to hear one word," Soren mumbled through clenched teeth. "I told you Titus was impressive."

"I won't say anything," Julian said, lifting both hands in the air.

Neither spoke as they waited patiently for Elin to finish pulling the last pieces from his back. She wiped the blood off the table, washed the open wounds, and double-checked the largest gash. The silence continued until she let out an overdramatic sigh.

"It's one thing after another today. Don't bother saying it. I know better than to stick around when you two walk into a room." She smacked Soren on the shoulder and ignored his grunt. "You're on your own, big guy."

She dumped the blood-coated glass in the garbage, the instruments and tray into the sink, then disappeared out the door. The stillness continued.

Preparing to get the ball rolling, he stretched the kink in his neck. "I take it you're not here to check on me."

"Gustav's here," Navarre said, going straight to the point.

"What?" Not good. Balinese might hold the reputation for being a peaceful city, but even so, no one would accept Gustav's type. "Has anyone seen him?"

"Only Steffen. He claims he has a message for me. The council meets in ten minutes," Navarre said. "Do you know what this is about?"

He shook his head. "Gustav hates people. I don't know why he would be here. We haven't spoken since I left Paris."

"He might be better behaved with you beside him," Navarre said.

"Let me change, and I'll be right there." Soren slid off the table, reaching for his duffel bag as Navarre left the room with Julian on his heels.

A short while later, freshly patched, and wearing his spare clothes, Soren walked into an uneasy council room. Every member watched Gustav like a hawk.

Captain Savard was the exception. Though the captain position himself at Lord Navarre's side, he wore the same bored expression as the last meeting. Gustav, on the other hand, was eating this up. He seemed to like creating restlessness among these vampires.

"Gustav." Soren reached out to his friend as he sat beside him.

He grasped Soren's forearm.

"We're all present, so let's begin," Navarre said. "I assume this message is from your lord?"

"It is, and I don't want to stay here long, so pay attention. I don't repeat myself. Demons have popped up all over the city. Our guess is over fifty, but they're hard to track. They haven't done much pack hunting, and we've rarely caught them feeding, but they're very comfortable roaming the city. Those not feeding appear to be searching for something in Paris." He slouched into his chair and rested his head back. "That's it. That's the message."

"I told you she'd bring them here," Vidor said, pointing a slender finger at Soren.

"She? Wait a minute." Gustav held his hands up, laughing. "Demons are searching for something other than people in Paris, and you think they want...what's her name? Faye. Fanny. Oh, for God's sake, Soren, what's the girl's name?"

"Faith."

"Yeah, her. You think they want her? You people just make this stuff up, don't you?" Gustav slapped his knee as he continued to roar with laughter.

"Soren took the human from them." Vidor said, as if all was explained.

The humor fizzled out of Gustav, and he leaned forward in his chair, his attention fixed on Vidor. "Let me educate you. No demon, alone or in a pack, would hunt down an escaped meal. Another bite to eat is always around the next corner. Trust me, they do not want Faith."

Soren released a breath he'd held as he'd listened intently to Gustav. She was safe. They weren't after Faith.

"You don't know what they're looking for, do you?" Navarre asked, studying Gustav.

"No. And since their searches are random, we don't even have a guess,"Gustav said.

"They must be looking for our cities," Julian offered.

"What else can they be looking for?" Bareth wondered, shrugging his hefty shoulders.

"Have you warned any of the other cities?" Navarre asked.

Gustav took a deep breath, clearly annoyed with all the questions. "No. My lord claims he is not the world's keeper. If you want them warned, that's your call. He won't get involved because no one is actually is a danger. He's only warning Balinese because they seem to have come from this direction."

"Demon migration?" Bareth chuckled.

"Should we warn the other cities?" Julian asked, and everyone waited in silence to hear the lord's answer.

Navarre shook his head slowly. "I don't believe we have a problem at this point."

"But, my lord, what of Talvane?" Soren asked, and mumbles of agreements rippled through those gathered. "The Guardians of Talvane have always been high in number for the sole reason that the city is within Paris, but it could be found."

"Talvane is a true concern. Gustav?" Navarre prompted.

Gustav shrugged. "They haven't gone near it yet."

"Then my decision remains the same. We will not warn the cities. It's possible those creatures could've been chased from their homes. Our history is riddled with such instances, and theirs would be as well. I will not panic entire cities needlessly. Especially as we've had minimal communication between cities these past decades. We will step up the guard on our gates. Gustav, will you send us word of any change in the demon searches?"

"I doubt I'll have a choice," he huffed.

Chapter 13

BALINESE

Faith walked down the hall, her boots hitting the stone floor in a solid rhythm. She had a purpose. She'd never been as emotionally unhinged as she was today, and she regretted being rude to Elin. She deserved an apology.

Cracking open the door, she peered in. Elin stood at a sink and tossed a handful of bloodied tools into water.

Faith might be clinging to her grudge against Soren, but she hoped that wasn't his blood. She gave the door a couple raps. "Excuse me, doctor?"

"Doctor? I'm not even a nurse," Elin said, flashing her an amused smile.

Okay, back to not liking this woman. "Then how did you get this position?"

"I can sew." Honest pride filled her voice.

"That's the extent of your qualifications? Sewing?"

"Truly, I don't want this for my life." Elin laughed, but after Faith's combative glare, threw her hands up in defeat. "Listen, take it easy. My father is the doctor and the surgeon. It's a family thing I've sort of been chin-deep in since I was a child. I handle the day to day normal, and Dad gets the surgical stuff. It's not like our kind die that often, anyway. Soren was perfectly safe."

A reasonable explanation. She hadn't actually considered what kind of medical attention a vampire would require. Luckily, it was minimal. "I thought I was helping him. I didn't know I would make it worse. I'm sorry."

With a short smile, she turned to leave.

"Why don't you sleep with him and get it over with?" Elin asked.

Faith stopped, sputtered, then finally spit out a distorted, "What?"

"You want him. He wants you. It's a simple equation."

It didn't get much more blunt than that. "I don't know what you're talking about."

"I've waited my whole life for a man to look at me the way Soren looks at you. He's a good man," Elin said as she rinsed off the bloody tweezers.

"He's not exactly a man." She couldn't stop staring at the pinkish-red water falling from Elin's fingers.

"He didn't choose to become vampire, he was born to it. He can't help what he is any more than you can help being human." Elin turned, pointed a soapy, accusing finger at her. "And you didn't seem to mind him being vampire when he had his teeth sunk into your neck, did you?"

Unable to answer her question, Faith turned and left, closing the door loudly behind her. The truth was, she hadn't minded at all. She'd enjoyed his bite, and that unnerved her more than anything.

She'd imagined the worst, a brutal puncture and severed veins, but it had been nothing more than a sweet sting. Not frightening in the least. And then with his talented lips he tugged gently, taking what he needed, building her desire with each little pull. If she'd had any strength left, she would have turned her head and offered the other side. Chilled hands pressed to her face, she cooled her cheeks.

After Julian had announced he needed blood, she'd been shaken, and ignored Soren's protests. That, or deep down she didn't want to hear them. Maybe part of her needed to experience exactly what she might be getting into with him.

She'd practically demanded he bite her. Though she'd been fully aware of him at her neck, she only remembered a hazy bliss.

Once inside Soren's home, she made a beeline to the bathroom mirror. The large mirror caught her image from mid-thigh on up. A muted blush covered her cheeks, and a tiny smile turned up the corners of her lips. The bite had mostly healed, leaving behind a couple reddish marks on her skin.

A twinge of guilt hit her. She'd been holding back, terrified he would hurt her with something more devastating than his bite. She should let go and let it happen, like Elin suggested.

A cool draft crossed her shoulders and goose bumps spread over her arms. Faith looked around. Where had it come from? The city had been built completely underground. Windows didn't exist here.

In the dresser, she dug through the clothes until she found her favorite blue sweatshirt. While zipping it, the cold air hit her again. She shot over to the thermostat. Seventy degrees. Plenty warm.

Through the perfectly still air, that chilling breeze brushed across her skin again, almost like a gust in the wake of someone passing by. How could that happen? She was alone.

She shivered, darting glances here and there. The cool air seemed to follow her around the room, and she couldn't shake the uneasiness building in her gut. Her skin positively crawled, and not because of the cold. She had a creepy feeling that the walls watched her.

The door opened and Soren walked through. The cool air suddenly dissipated, which did nothing to soothe her ramped-up fears. She ran to him.

"Faith?" When she launched herself into his arms, he dropped his bag and held her, crooning gently, "What's this, now?"

"Where were you?" she asked, clinging to him.

"Meeting with the council. Why?" He tried to pull them apart to look at her face, but she couldn't let go.

"Something's in here," she whispered.

He stilled. "Why would you think that?"

"There can't be drafts in here, it's not possible, but I kept feeling cool breezes. And I could have sworn someone was watching me. I wanted you here," she rambled, then tucked her head under his chin.

His muscles grew rigid against her. She peeked at him from her haven and anxiousness returned. With frightening intensity, he searched the room.

"How long ago?" he asked quietly.

"Just now. What's wrong?"

"Do you see the red button on the wall there, by the thermostat?"

"Yes." She'd noticed the odd waist level placement of the button, but hadn't asked, assuming it was a fire alarm.

"If that happens again, especially being cold, push that button. It will call the Guardians to this room. You'll be protected. When they arrive, tell them everything. Can you do that for me?"

She nodded. If the cold air upset Soren enough to map out emergency procedures, then this was bad. "What was in here?"

Soren continued to scan the room as he whispered, "When a vampire takes their Spirit form, they become invisible, like a living ghost. A Spirit can walk through walls and locked doors. They can go anywhere without being seen or detected, but when their body is in Spirit, it's colder than the air around them. The person, their Spirit, is that cold air."

"Someone was watching me?"

"Possibly, but I can't think of who or why. I don't like this. I can't fight what I can't see." He growled his frustration, then focused on her and cradled her face in his hands. "I refuse to sugarcoat the situation for you. This scares the hell out of me. I don't want you leaving my side. If you do, you'll be guarded."

She nodded, in complete agreement with him.

"We're going to find Captain Savard. Right now." He took her hand, and together they left his home.

They hadn't gone far when they came across Navarre leaning on the railing overlooking the pond. He turned as he heard their approach.

"Have you seen Captain Savard?" Soren asked from a distance.

"He never lets me enjoy my pond alone," Navarre said with a grin, then pointed to his left. "He's right around the corner."

The captain stepped into view, his hand settled on his sword hilt.

"There was a damn Spirit in my home," Soren said in a growling tone.

Captain Savard darted down the hall and disappeared into Soren's home.

Navarre straightened, a dark shadow crossing his face. "You're certain?"

"No," Soren admitted. "I have no proof. Faith was alone, but what she described had no other explanation than a Spirit."

Captain Savard emerged, shaking his head slowly. "There's nothing now. Damn, I hate chasing Spirits."

"Thank God few can change." Navarre rubbed his chin, slipping off into thought.

"You sure you didn't see anyone?" Captain Savard asked her.

"I'm sure. Just cold breezes and a creepy feeling," she admitted, relieved that they took her seriously, because to her ears, she sounded like a crazy person.

"She didn't see anything, Soren." Captain Savard slid his fingers through his dark hair, clearly frustrated. "I can't do a lot with only a description of 'cold breeze' to go on."

"I could post Guardians at your door," Navarre mused. "It won't accomplish much if this person can take Spirit."

"No. Balinese needs Guardians at the gate." Soren shook his head. "Just add a man to patrol this end for a day or two."

Though his mind seemed otherwise occupied, the captain nodded sharply. "Done."

As the captain's eyes settled on her, she leaned on Soren. Concern hadn't left Savard's young features from the moment he'd taken off and searched Soren's home.

Lord Navarre obviously recognized that look. "What is it, Captain? Can you find a Spirit?"

"No, but walking in Spirit would weaken even a strong vampire. What I can find is a worn out bastard who needs to feed," the captain said with a determined nod, now on a mission.

―――――――――

Soren's weight settled onto the mattress, and Faith rolled, threw her arm over his stomach and pressed her face against his shoulder. He lifted his arm, and she snuggled closer to his side. She needed him to hold her.

Though she clung to his warm, bare chest, the heat of his body wasn't enough. She shivered once, twice, then tugged the blanket over her shoulders.

"What...what is it?" he mumbled, half asleep.

"Cold," she murmured.

He shifted sharply, jarring her awake. A pained masculine cry rang through the room, drowning out her sleepy protests.

"Soren?" Afraid he'd been hurt, she reached out. What had happened? He didn't answer her, and when she found his face in the dimly lit room, his murderous gaze stared past her. Oh, God, it hadn't been Soren who'd cried out.

Sword hilt clenched in his hand, Faith followed the sharp blade to its end. The sword's tip had sunk deep inside a man with glowing red eyes.

Loud and long, she screamed. Petrifaction set in, and she watched in horror as the man reached for her. Each time his hand stretched toward her, Soren's blade went further through his shoulder. The sword wasn't stopping him.

Soren lunged over her, left her alone in the center of the bed and pushed the red-eyed man away from her. No, he wasn't a man. This was a demon.

The demon fought wildly, twisting himself sharply to gain the upper hand. Soon both men crashed to the floor. The sword followed with a muffled thud. A head rose above the level of the mattress, an elbow, but she couldn't decipher who belonged to what.

Suddenly they were upright, on their feet for a second round. She couldn't separate them in the dark. One threw the other against the wall. Hard. For a moment, everything went still.

Soren pinned the demon to the wall, but her sense that everything would now turn out fine shattered as the creature smiled, fangs gleaming. Its red eyes found her in the dark.

Soren slammed his fist against the demon's face. Breaking her contact with the demon, he then drove his fist into its injured shoulder. The demon howled.

"Faith!" His strained voice yanked her focus back on him. "Push the button."

She flew off the bed and across the room, smacking the button. Nothing happened. No lights, no sirens. Two more times, then she flattened her back against the wall.

Her eyes adjusted to the darkness, and she was able to make out both men. Soren punched the demon, his fist landing heavily on the creature's jaw. It sent the demon to the floor. Then both dove after the sword.

Faith bit her lip. Through grunts, growls, and muffled punches, she waited silently. She refused to be the distraction that could cost Soren his life.

The door burst open, and the light from the hallway caught Soren's bare back. Then everything around her moved in slow motion.

Five or six men ran into the room, not one of them paying her any heed. Soren had his hands around the demon's throat, and it took everyone present to separate him from the demon. Or had it been the other way around? The rest of the men swarmed around the demon.

Two Guardians wrestled with Soren, doing their best to keep him at bay. More than once he'd struggled to break free and finish off the demon.

"Hit an artery!" someone yelled.

Who gave the command, she didn't know, but they quickly obeyed. Then a flash of steel glinted.

Within several seconds the demon sagged, leaning on the Guardians for support. They locked their arms around the creature and hauled it out the door, having no choice but to take the demon past her.

They came near her, and it lunged for her, gleaming red eyes flaring brighter. She cried out, instinctively covering her face. A Guardian stepped between them and punched the demon with the hilt of his sword, disorienting the creature and preventing it from touching her.

She slid to the floor, closed her eyes, and hugged her knees to her chest. Her body shook, but she wasn't cold. Not anymore.

In one violent twist, Soren threw the men off him and ran to Faith. She shuddered and cried, rocking back and forth, gaze fixed on the floor.

Kneeling before Faith, he pushed her hair off her face, stroking her cheeks as he spoke. "Look at me, Faith. I need you to look at me."

She finally did, and with a choked sob, threw herself at him, wrapped her arms tightly around his neck as her tears fell.

"It's gone, Faith. We're going somewhere else tonight," he said softly, but she didn't acknowledge him.

He stroked her hair, the soothing, slow rhythm doing them both a world of good.

"Soren," Captain Savard held out his hand, a single key in the center of his palm. "Take my home. I won't be returning tonight."

"I owe you, Captain," he said, then scooped Faith up fast and carried her away.

The captain's home was close by, and Soren didn't bother turning on the lights as he entered. Not wanting to risk damaging any progress he'd made in calming her, he avoided the bed, and sat in an overstuffed chair and cradled her on his lap, rocking her gently.

He rested his cheek against her soft hair, his shoulder absorbing her broken sobs. If he hadn't awakened to her mumbling about the cold, she would be dead. The thought chilled him. He had no desire to live without her.

In an effort to calm himself, he breathed deeply. She was here in his arms. Her human life was fragile, but she lived. He had a sudden urge to bite his arm and force her to drink from him. Being vampire would give her a greater chance of survival, and he wanted that for her. Badly.

But he couldn't do it. Unless they were first mated, the act was punishable by death. Besides, judging by the way she'd gaped at him when the Guardians separated him from the demon, he doubted she would enjoy being bound to him forever. He hadn't just been defending himself. He'd had every intention of ripping that demon apart. When the Guardians tore the demon away, he'd been pissed.

She'd seen the whole thing, his murderous focus, the rage within him, the power to kill viciously.

"I'm sorry, Faith," he whispered. "You're right. I am an animal."

Head raised, she studied his face. The tracks of her tears caught the dim light. "The demon would have killed us if you'd been anything other than what you are," she said, her lower lip quivering.

"You weren't scared?"

"Out of my mind scared," she said, and Soren turned his face away. She wouldn't let him, took his cheeks between her hands and guided him to her. "I was afraid he'd kill you."

"None of this should have happened. If I were not vampire, I wouldn't have bitten you in the streets or kidnapped you. You would never have known that creature existed." He shook his head, unable to look her in the eye.

"Maybe not, but I'd be dead in an alley if not for you. I see how much you care for the people around you, and I understand why you brought me here. This is not your fault." She curled up on his chest, her tears streaming anew. "I wish I knew why he came for me."

Her tears soaked through his shirt, burning his skin. "It wasn't trying to kill you."

"Then why did he..." Her eyes grew wide, the look in them, fearful. "He was there to kill you? Why?"

Careful not to jostle her, he shrugged his right shoulder lightly. "We won't know unless the demon explains its actions."

"Teach me," she demanded, chin set stubbornly.

Soren cocked his head. "Teach you what?"

"Anything. Show me how to shoot a gun, or use my knife."

"Why?"

"I pushed a damn button, Soren. A button. I couldn't physically do anything to save your life." Another tear slid down her cheek, but the weeping had stopped. Now she was angry. "I hatred being helpless."

He searched her eyes, adoring the courage he saw in her. "I didn't think you had any desire to be one of my...what did you call them?"

"Warrior women."

"Change you mind, did you?" He relished the fact that preserving his life triggered her determination.

"You brought a sword to bed. That's the kind of world I live in now. You need to bring me up to speed," she said with a sharp nod.

He chuckled. "I promise."

He couldn't soothe her fears, because they were real. However, he would use the literal arsenal at his disposal to give her confidence and peace of mind.

Chapter 14

═══

BALINESE

The decorative pale blue walls seemed odd, but not as out of place as the white carpet. Not a single light had been switched on and yet the whole place practically glowed. She hadn't expected Captain Savard to have a home this beautiful and pristine.

Sometime after she'd fallen asleep, Soren had someone bring in a change of clothes for them and had moved her to the bed. Even in sleep, sprawled on his belly, he'd kept his arm wrapped around her. She rolled away, his hand flopping onto the mattress the moment she gained freedom. He didn't wake.

She went in search of the bathroom. Her puffy eyes and tear-coated cheeks wanted the soothing shower spray. A similar theme of pale blue walls with white and gold trim flowed into Captain Savard's bathroom. The distant, cool blue color matched the captain, but the wealthy image his home projected, did not.

Sitting on the edge of the tub, she yanked off her socks, and waited for the water to warm. The bathroom door swung open and Soren walked in without making any excuses. He simply closed the toilet lid and sat.

"I'm taking a shower," she said, shooing him away. He didn't budge. "Get out."

"I'm not leaving you alone." He leaned back, shifting to find a comfortable position.

"You don't need to sit in the bathroom. Go out there and I'll leave the door open a crack."

"I'm staying here," he said firmly.

She narrowed her eyes on him a brief moment, then climbed into the shower, clothes and all, and tugged the striped curtain closed. The swish of fabric hadn't sounded as angry as she'd anticipated. Once her wet clothes were off, she threw them over the top of the curtain, aiming for Soren. He didn't say a word, but she truly hoped she'd hit him. Stubborn man.

The hot water poured over her, but she didn't have the luxury of a long and relaxing shower. The conversation she wanted to have with him wouldn't happen if she were soaking wet and under water. She washed and dried herself quickly.

Soren being parked outside the shower, a few feet away, seemed overkill. He had every right to act edgy after what had happened, but something about it had burrowed under his skin.

She stuck her arm out, palm up. "Give me my pants."

The heavy weight landed in her hand and she pulled them on, a tricky feat in a slippery tub.

"Shirt," she prompted, then snatched it from him after it appeared. "I realize I don't know demons like you do, but I doubt they'll start popping out of the walls. He's dead, Soren. He can't hurt me."

"It's not dead," he said, his voice flat.

"What?" She threw the curtain open. "I saw him get stabbed. He lost a lot of blood. I thought they killed him."

"You look nice," he said with a smile.

Dang it, she'd got her arms through her shirtsleeves, but hadn't finished pulling it over her head. She chose to ignore her state of undress. "Why didn't they kill him? You killed the ones in Paris."

"We protect an entire city, which makes things different down here. The Guardians bled the demon to weaken it, then locked it away. Savard likely questioned it throughout the day. Tonight it will be executed."

"Executed?" Wow, they worked fast.

"Faith, I know this will be hard for you." He paused before adding, "You'll be at the execution."

"I have to watch that thing die?"

"Watch as much as you can, but you must be there. This is our way of life, and it will not change."

Well, that certainly ended the conversation. She flipped on her hairdryer and closed her eyes.

The demon being alive and somewhere in the city made her jumpy, but finding *attend execution* on her to do list for the day scared the living daylights out of her.

He should have told her, prepared her to face the demon again. Or had she been better off not knowing?

If he'd told her the demon lived last night, she wouldn't have slept a wink. She switched off the hairdryer and set it on the floor. Soren hadn't moved. "I know why you didn't tell me, but I wish you would have."

He nodded, a touch of sadness and regret in his expression, then said softly, "I didn't know how."

A knock at the door interrupted them and had Soren moving swiftly. Captain Savard waited patiently outside his home.

"It's time," the captain said.

"Already?" she asked, and Soren gestured for her to join them. A lump lodged in her stomach, twisting.

His fingers splayed wide over the small of her back as he placed her between him and the captain.

They made the short journey in silence, and as the chattering ahead grew louder, Soren asked, "Did it say anything?"

"No." Captain Savard surveyed the crowd entering through two massive, arched doors with wrought iron hinges, handles, and mirrored curling designs.

Instead of melding with the crowd, she continued on with Soren and Savard to an average sized door.

"What's in there?" she asked the captain.

"Lord Navarre's private box," the captain answered, allowing them to enter before him.

A set of steeply angled stone stairs loomed before her. She reached out to Soren and he clasped her hand, kept her steady as they climbed together.

"What's a private box?" she whispered to Soren.

Captain Savard answered, his voice tinged with revulsion, "Think of it as going to the opera. Box seats are the best in the house."

She didn't want the best seat for this.

Light flooded the small landing at the top of the stairs that opened into an enclosed, bi-level room made from the same gray stones as the stairwell.

Royal blue curtains and gold sashes lined the room, covering the stone walls and creating a more refined atmosphere. Three beautifully fashioned stone seats ran across the upper level, and three matching ones filled the lower. Even stuffed full of colorful pillows, each seat would easily be wide enough for two people.

Lord Navarre sat in the center of the first row, and as he saw them, quickly rose, his hand extended to Soren.

"I am pleased to see you are well, my friend," Lord Navarre said, and they grasped each other's forearm in their own version of a handshake. "And Faith, how are you?"

She gave him an unsteady smile. "I'm fine."

"Good. Come with me." Navarre took her hand and led her to the seat at his right.

Soren settled next to her, but stunned and at a complete loss for words, she gazed out on a vision that could have been torn from ancient Rome.

Pale sand stretched out like a wavy sea contained by a solid, circular wall. The wall stood a dozen feet or more tall and formed the barrier between the crowd and the spectacle below.

Above the wall, the first two rows of vampires sat on brightly colored pillows. The rest sat on bare stone, thousands of them watching the sand. Waiting.

This place had obviously been designed to keep something trapped inside. Two doors had been set several feet into the wall opposite each other, one on her left, and the other to her right. The old and abused fat wooden boards were riddled with deep gouges.

Gripping the stone edge of her seat, she straightened, leaned forward. This was a bullfight, an unfair battle between a capable matador and a weakened animal. Did they enjoy this kind of entertainment?

The captain lingered at the top of the stairs they'd come through, making no attempt to sit, watch, or enter the box. His gaze avoided the sand. Navarre, on the other hand, seemed to drink in the experience, savor the event. And Soren? His focus was glued on the door to the left, no doubt the same one the demon would come through.

"What is this place?" she asked, almost afraid of the answer.

"This is the arena. We built the arena, then we built Balinese around it," Navarre answered. Each breath he took lifted his proud shoulders.

"How long ago?" she asked.

"After the Romans built their Colosseum," Navarre hinted with a smile.

"So you built this for death and sport." She glared at him.

"No, Faith," Navarre said, looking disappointed, the pride gone from his face. "People have and will continue to die in this arena, but the purpose is justice. Always justice."

"Then does he get a trail?"

"It does, though the verdict is clear." Navarre pointed across the sands at a group of seats sectioned off to his right where five men sat. "You would normally sit there, but human rights down here is a tricky subject, therefore you will not give testimony. Those five men are the Guardians who saved your lives, and will be the witness for this trial."

The crowd shouted and jeered as two Guardians escorted the demon into the arena, prodding him along from behind with their swords. Inky black blood covered the demon's clothes and his slow steps dragged shallow tracks in the sand.

The Guardians brought him to the center of the arena, pulled two chains from the sand, and shackled the demon's legs in place. She covered her mouth. He looked like a man, an ordinary, exhausted man with red eyes.

Soren tucked her close and whispered, "I'm right here, Faith. It can't have you."

She grabbed his hand, drawing on him for strength.

Lord Navarre stood and walked to the ledge. In a loud, commanding tone, he addressed the five men he'd pointed out to her a moment ago. "Witnesses, let one speak for all. Where did you find this demon?"

One man stood, replying, "In the home of Soren Rayner."

His testimony likely having confirmed several rumors, gasps rippled through the crowd.

"And what did you see?" Lord Navarre asked.

"The demon attempted to kill Soren, and when it failed, it tried to kill Soren's woman as we took it from his home." She thought the Guardian had finished, but he spoke once more. "We had no other choice but to bleed the demon. It had no intention of leaving without taking a life."

An odd vocal mix rose from the people around them. Some whispered, putting their heads together, while others shouted out their opinions.

Navarre faced the creature, and his voice rang through the arena. "Demon, you and your kind are not permitted to enter Balinese, or any vampire city. Yet here you stand. Not only did you break our law, but also you attempted murder. Twice. Have you anything to say?"

The demon only smiled, his fangs glinting as they caught the light.

"Entering our cities will not be tolerated, and attempted murder is punishable by death. You have broken two sacred laws. This is my city. Live by my laws or die." The arena fell silent as Navarre paused. No one moved, no one breathed. "You, demon, have chosen death."

The door to her right opened, and wild cheering rose in a roar around her. Bareth stepped into the arena wielding a large broadsword. Navarre's words ricocheted through her mind at the sight of the polished metal.

"Is he...is Bareth going to kill him?"

"He is," Soren said evenly.

Bareth approached the condemned man cautiously. Though he remained shackled, the demon scanned the arena with his red eyes, then fixed them on Bareth. Tipping his chin up, the demon braced for death.

Bareth drove his blade through the demon's chest, straight through the heart. For a moment, the demon stood and stared. Then his lips moved as if he spoke to Bareth. With a short jerk, he pulled the sword from the demon's body and it crumpled, the thirsty sand drinking in the fresh blood.

It was done.

Faith turned away, pressed her cheek against Soren's chest. The violence and the slicing jab of Bareth's sword had been hard to watch, but she'd needed the closure. As the tension ebbed from his shoulders, Soren's hold on her became less crushing. He'd needed this, too.

"Soren..." Navarre leaned forward, studying the scene before him.

On the sands below, Bareth stood absolutely still, the kind of stillness that suspended time. He stared at the black blood on the end of his blade, then slowly, looked up to Navarre. Bareth turned away, heading for the door. He took only a handful of steps, then peered over his shoulder at the fallen demon.

Soren stood at her side. Something was wrong.

"Captain, Soren, go to Bareth. Now," Navarre ordered. Captain Savard had already sprung into motion, vanishing down the stairwell.

Soren hesitated, still holding her hand.

"She's safe with me. Go," Navarre commanded. Soren squeezed her hand, then darted after the captain.

"What's wrong?" she asked quietly.

"I don't know," he answered her, but without turning his head or physically acknowledging the man's presence, called, "Sampson?"

"Yes, my lord?" the man said, remaining hidden, probably in the folds of the thick curtains.

She remembered Sampson. He'd been the only Guardian to knock Soren on his ass. A skilled man like him hidden at his lord's side eased her mind.

"I want Nero and Steffen here." Navarre searched the slowly dispersing crowd.

Sampson spoke again, but not to Navarre. Faith couldn't make out the words.

"Steffen is..." Sampson had paused, or maybe his voice had faltered. "Nero and Flynn are on their way."

Not more than a minute later, a man she recognized appeared from the stairway, then another familiar face followed on his heels.

"My lord?" the first man asked.

"Nero, Flynn, this is Faith," Navarre introduced them. "She is Soren's woman. Guard her with your lives."

Both men nodded and immediately flanked her.

"I don't like this at all," she whispered.

"Neither do I." Navarre's focus had already been relocated to the door through which Bareth had exited.

What would worry the Lord of Balinese to this extent? She couldn't see it. The crowd talked happily among themselves as they shuffled into the aisles on their way home. Unaware.

"Bareth?" Captain Savard asked, cautiously approaching his High Justice so as not to startle him.

Bareth remained silent, staring at the floor, a hand covering his mouth.

"What happened?" Soren asked calmly, stepping into his line of sight.

"We made a mistake. We made a terrible mistake." Bareth shook his head as if still trying to sort things out.

Captain Savard stopped short. "Should we not have killed the demon?"

"Oh, no, it had to die." Bareth fell silent for a long moment, then returned his focus to Soren. "We were right. They're looking for our cities."

The captain cursed, the sound echoing off the tunnel wall. Soren walked right up to Bareth. "How do you know?"

Bareth reached out and gripped his shoulders. "With my sword buried deep in its chest, it said 'It begins with me. Now watch your people die.'"

"A dying man wanting the last word." Captain Savard shook his head.

"No," Bareth whispered, a haunted look in his eyes. "I have seen many deaths, heard many last words and prayers. This was different. It had no fear in its eyes, only absolute certainty. Like it knew when and how it would defeat us. Like its death was a signal."

Chapter 15

BALINESE

Soren had retrieved her from Nero and Flynn and sent the Guardians where they would be put to better use. Now she walked between him and Gustav, her arm looped around his, and once again guarded by two men.

He had plenty of reasons to worry about her safety. Gustav agreed, and planned on staying in Balinese to watch over Faith for the next few nights while Soren helped the captain. Having the alert and wary Stalker in his home would be a relief.

"How's Bareth? What happened?" Faith asked.

Soren took a deep breath, then let it out slowly. He'd waited for this question. "He's fine. The demon gave a prophecy before Bareth killed it."

"What kind of prophecy?"

"It foretold the end of the vampire race. It takes a great deal to shake Bareth, and Navarre is taking every precaution," Soren said.

"Does what the demon said really matter if he's dead?"

"Navarre won't take any chances. Captain Savard and I have started organizing Guardians for a possible attack. I don't know if it will help. I feel more worn out than prepared." He brought her hand to his lips, kissed her knuckles.

"And I was so happy to help, by the way." Gustav sent Soren an irritated smirk, then grumbled, "I can't believe I'm stuck here."

"Navarre asked you to stay for a couple days. You're the one who said yes." Sympathy was unneeded. Gustav's sarcastic comments veiled a genuine concern.

Faith giggled. "At least you'll have a great sleep. Even a couch would be better than your bed. I've slept on that thing, and..."

He and Gustav held up their hands to silence her and she shut her mouth and held still. The door to his home had been left wide open.

Without a word, Gustav pulled his sword free and disappeared through the open door alone. Soren pulled Faith to his side, gun in hand, and waited for Gustav to return. The deafening silence worked his nerves, tumbling possibilities through his mind.

Gustav reappeared and shook his head slowly. "Go have a look."

"Did someone break in?" she whispered to Gustav.

"Not exactly," he said, and stood rigid, gaze glued on the doorway. Not a good sign.

"Stay here," Soren said low, and left her with Gustav.

The demon blood the Guardians had spilled last night had been removed from the carpet. He'd asked the servants to eliminate any trace of the demon, and after they'd finished, made a point of verifying that it was ready for Faith to come home. The room had been spotless before someone made this mess.

A lamp had been knocked over, and a vase from the dresser had shattered on the floor. Strange.

One of her small silver hoop earrings had fallen onto the floor, which he picked up. No damage. No theft. Things at arm level had been tossed around, scattered like someone had left in anger. His empty home had made someone extremely disappointed.

He didn't want Faith anywhere near this place. Stepping over the lamp, he reached for the silent alarm on the wall.

Before he could touch it, the city's alarm sounded. The siren rang through his home and the hallways, as it would throughout Balinese.

———————

Soren ran out the door, gun in one hand and his sword in the other. Something was seriously wrong. She'd jumped when the alarm blared, and Gustav had cursed repeatedly. But Soren? He'd emerged unruffled, almost as if he'd switched into Guardian mode.

"And that noise is?" Gustav yelled above the blaring alarm.

"It can only be set off by a Guardian. We're under attack." Soren checked his gun, then handed it to Gustav. "Take her to the arena."

"No! I want to stay with you," she cried.

"Navarre is the heart of this city. If he dies, the city is lost. I have to protect him." Soren kissed her soundly, then pushed her toward Gustav. "Take her. Go."

Gustav hooked his arm around her and forced her to move. He'd taken her away from Soren so fast, she hadn't seen which way he'd gone. It didn't matter. She couldn't follow him. Gustav had a fierce hold on her.

Together they wove through the vampires, somehow always moving against them. Gustav sheltered her from the panicked people flooding the hallways.

"What's in the arena?" she asked, her voice barely audible above the alarm.

"Protection," Gustav said, never slowing.

They turned the corner sharply, and she lost her footing. Gustav righted her, bumping into another man in the process. They kept moving.

More men darted past them, leaving only a few in the corridor. If the arena equaled safety, then why weren't more people here?

At her side, Gustav constantly searched the faces of those surrounding them. He'd noticed it, too.

"Move faster," he snapped.

She ran. Fear of the unknown kept her moving. The alarm vibrated through her, interfered with the pounding rhythm of her heart. They were almost there. The arena doors were just ahead.

"Run," Gustav yelled. Then suddenly he released her, shoved her forward.

Her body slammed hard against the arena door, jolting her teeth. The air left her lungs in a huff, and she let the door support her as she caught her breath.

She spun around to find Gustav. He lay face down on the ground, Soren's gun several feet from his hand, and a red-eyed man stood over him. The demon pried its sword from Gustav's back, blood coating the blade.

Faith screamed. A stupid and thoughtless action, but she couldn't stop. Gustav's lifeless eyes still stared in her direction. Tears fell freely, blurring her vision. Gustav shouldn't be dead. It wasn't right. It wasn't fair.

Those red eyes turned on her, and she screamed again. Not daring to turn her back on the creature, she pounded on the door behind her with the side of her fist.

The demon stalked her with a sinister smile, unconcerned with his surroundings. Blade lowered, he focused on her, his prey.

"Hello, human." The demon licked his lips, making a show of baring his fangs.

An icy chill surrounded her for only a moment, then she felt the solid length of a man at her back, and his thick arm encircled her. The demon stopped its advance and raised his blade. Who had her, she didn't know, but he must be vampire.

"This one's not for you, Red," the man behind her said.

The demon charged them. The solid objects around her became hazy. Her head spun, and she couldn't tell up from down. Her stomach churned and muscles quivered like jelly, but it only lasted for a moment.

"Faith," the man said, bowing his head slightly. "I trust your short travel in Spirit wasn't too uncomfortable."

"Titus?" she asked, and he gave her a lopsided grin, confirming his identity.

Dyre came to stand at her side, and guided her away from the doors into the center of the arena. They slipped through a ring of Guardians, and then a circle of men. In the center, a multitude of women looked as frightened as she felt. Even so, they stood their ground, swords held awkwardly before them.

The cool hilt of a sword landed in her hand, and she opened her mouth to protest, but Dyre hadn't placed it there. He'd already gone. Elin stood at her side, gripping a narrow blade expertly.

"What do we do?" Faith scrubbed the lingering tears from her face and tightened both fists around the sword hilt. Like the other women, lifting the heavy sword was a challenge.

"We make sure no demon touches the children," Elin whispered, gaze fixed on the double doors.

Faith spun around. There, in the heart of the circle, children huddled together. They held hands, not making a peep. Sand shifted as the constantly vigilant Guardians moved around the men and women.

No longer was there a question of whether they might be attacked. It was a matter of when. She would have been more scared, but for the fact she wasn't alone. Behind her, innocent children depended on her for safety. Women stood alongside her, setting aside differences to join together and protect the children. Men and Guardians defended the lot of them. She wasn't an outsider here anymore, but part of them, one of them. She was home. And to save these people, she would do anything.

Faith prayed for Soren's safety. She missed him, wanted him by her side, craved the sense of security she'd come to rely on from him. Now she could only wonder. Had he found Navarre? Was he safe? Or had he been killed as easily as Gustav?

A sob threatened to escape, and she choked it down. Soren would want her to be strong, and she planned to make him proud.

Chapter 16

———

BALINESE

Soren warily eyed the twenty plus demons stalking toward them in the narrow corridor. He didn't like this, not their smiles nor their slow pace. His skin practically itched with apprehension. "Where's Navarre?"

"Headed to the council room, last I saw," Bareth answered, twisting his sword in his hand, impatient to split a demon in two.

"What?" Captain Savard snapped, grabbing Bareth's shirtsleeve in his fist. "I left him in the arena. Was Sampson with him?"

"No." Bareth shook his head slowly, then his jaw dropped, as if he'd just realized what his words meant.

"He'll be trapped," Captain Savard whispered. The demons were no longer important. "Nero, Soren, Flynn. Come with me. Bareth, take command."

"Yes, sir," Bareth smiled with eager anticipation.

"Guardians!" Captain Savard's voice echoed down the halls. "Follow Bareth. He will bring justice this day."

The Guardians roared their acceptance even as Captain Savard moved through his men with the chosen three on his heels.

"For Balinese!" Bareth yelled.

"Balinese!" the Guardians behind him roared in response.

Once they'd cleared the Guardians, Soren and the three men with him vanished, took their Spirit forms and they raced through walls and earth. This was the shortest route to the council room. One corridor, one waiting room, a short hallway and they would be there.

Captain Savard released his Spirit in the waiting room, and ran.

"Captain?" Steffen's voice came over the captain's radio.

Captain Savard cursed as he answered the call, running with a sword in one hand and now a radio in the other. Soren and the other Guardians ran behind him, their footfalls heavy, determined.

"I'm a little busy," the captain replied, nearly growling.

"I see red eyes. Demons are in the woods," Steffen said.

"How many?"

"Ten. Fifteen, maybe." The radio crackled, but between the static Steffen said one clear word: "Coming."

"Hold your ground!" Captain Savard shouted into the radio as they rounded the corner. They were mere feet from the council room. "Do you hear me, Steffen? Hold your ground! Don't let those vermin through our gates!"

"I thought they'd already breached the gates," Soren said, dread curling in his stomach.

The radio went dead.

Captain Savard threw open the doors to the council room and they charged inside. Empty. It was empty.

"Damn. Find him!" their captain yelled as he ran back out the door.

"How?" Nero called after him.

"We try his rooms." Captain Savard surged forward, racing far ahead of his men.

Soren had never seen the captain so angry, or push himself so hard. He'd always been the levelheaded one, the crisis control, the solid ground. They needed their captain composed right now, as Guardians, and as men who had families somewhere in the city.

Not many had ever witnessed raw emotion from Captain Savard. Had the attack brought it out, or Navarre's disappearance?

They finally reached the secluded wing belonging to the Lord of Balinese. It was quiet, still. Soren feared they were too late.

"Navarre!" Captain Savard yelled, bursting into Navarre's home.

No answer, or any sound at all. Soren searched the adjoining rooms. Nothing.

"Oh, no. No!" Flynn's aggrieved cry tore through them. Soren's heart lurched. They ran to him, each step seeming sluggishly surreal.

Sampson lay on the floor, discarded, several gaping holes in his chest. In death, his fingers still clenched his bloodied sword. That he was not Navarre didn't make it any easier.

"If Sampson is dead...." Nero couldn't finish the sentence.

"They might already have him," Captain Savard finished for him.

"They might not," Soren said. He could barely catch a solid stream of though. Adrenaline was not always a good thing. "Navarre is smart. He's strong. What if he escaped?"

"Leaving Sampson?" Nero asked in disbelief.

"Maybe Sampson stayed as a decoy." Soren grasped for an explanation.

The captain shook his head with certainty. "Not on Navarre's orders."

"Navarre could be fighting," Flynn said quietly.

"Don't say that." Captain Savard combed his fingers through his hair roughly, anger seeping from him. "Damn you, don't you dare say that."

"Why? Why not say it?" Soren glared at the captain.

"Because he would!" the captain roared, shooting him a level stare.

Flynn looked near hopeless. "He could be anywhere."

"Captain?" Nero called in an anxious voice from the doorway.

They joined him, followed his gaze down the empty hallway.

Soren stepped into the corridor. Nothing. Then from his right came the faint clash of swords.

"To your lord!" Captain Savard yelled, bolting down corridor.

Soren followed, Flynn and Nero on his heels. They rounded the corner, and Soren carried too much momentum. He banked off the left wall. Here, in the corridor leading to the main entrance of the city, Navarre battled alone, holding off three demons.

Captain Savard heaved a demon off Navarre, neatly slicing its arm. The creature's flailing surprise made its heart an easy target. Soren and Nero took out the other two by stabbing them deep in their backs.

No time to catch their breath. Six more demons came from the city's dark entrance. Two went for Navarre, two more charged after the captain, completely ignoring the rest of the Guardians.

Nero intercepted a demon, as did Flynn. Soren aided Navarre, thrusting his blade through the ribs of a particularly tall one. It bellowed in anger. As he pulled his sword from the demon, it turned on him.

Soren ducked under the creature's sword arm and stabbed it in the ribs again. This time it faltered, went to its knees. Soren didn't waste the opportunity. He drove his fist into its face, knocked it on its back, and pierced it through the heart.

Nero and Flynn still fought the same demons, and the two after Captain Savard had backed him against the wall. They'd have to wait. Soren strode toward Navarre, intent on finishing off the threat to his lord.

A demon broke away from Captain Savard, barreled at Soren. Unlike the first demon he'd bested, this one was ready for him.

Their swords met. The heavy metal clatter echoed off the stone surrounding them. Soren threw his weight against the demon, pushed it back to gain ground. They broke apart, and his quick jabs were barely enough to keep the demon from getting too close.

Nero cried out, and Soren glanced in time to see his friend fall and the demon easily overpower him now that he was down. There was nothing he could do. Nero was already gone.

A sharp pain sliced along his bicep, and he poured out his anger through his sword, slamming it down hard on the demon, bombarding the foul creature's defenses. He had to kill it quickly. Nero's killer had set its sights on Navarre.

Captain Savard blocked a killing blow to Flynn, but paid for it with a deep gash to his side. With the enemy's next strike, Flynn fell, and as he did, the demon surged at Captain Savard.

Savard dropped to his knees, shoved his blade upward, into the assailant's rib cage. The demon dropped, and Savard rolled away, using the corpse to block a blow from a second demon.

This entire scenario felt...wrong. Every time a vampire went down, the enemy went for the captain or Navarre. They'd cornered the two men in command of the city, and they were well aware of that fact.

His attack became more aggressive, driving the demon back hard. With no choice but to step backward and catch its balance, it tripped over a body, then tumbled onto the floor. Soren speared his sword through its neck, then its chest.

The sudden crying and screaming of children muted the sounds of clashing metal. He whipped around, trying to pinpoint the origin.

"Savard!" Navarre shouted, pointing at the doorway to the chateau's cellar.

Captain Savard followed his direction, as did Soren. Farther up the corridor, six demons made their exit from the city, each carrying a child. Two of the younger girls had fathers right here, lying dead on the floor. The last demon held the youngest, a small toddler with short wispy curls and round, frightened eyes. She belonged to Sampson.

"No!" Captain Savard yelled as he dodged blow after blow from the demon. "You stay here."

"Get this filth out of my city, Captain," Navarre snapped as he shoved the demon, jabbed his sword deep in its gut. It fell, leaving only one for Soren. The Lord of Balinese sprinted after the children.

Soren drove his blade through his bleeding victim, then engaged the other, blocking it from following Navarre.

"Go, Captain! Help Navarre," Soren urged.

He glanced back. The demon lay dead and Captain Savard had already disappeared.

With renewed strength, Soren battered the last demon, and as he caught its shoulder, it howled in pain. Its arm hung, useless. He finished it, sending his sword through its heart.

Soren ripped off the end of his shirt, tied it tightly around his arm to stop his blood from oozing out. He stepped over the bodies of friends and foes, and made his way above. The door had been flung wide open.

As he dashed through the cellar and up the stairs, the hollow sound of every footfall ricocheted through the night. It shouldn't be this quiet.

He stepped from the kitchen and into the main room. The tall, arched windows cast fat moonlit stripes onto the floor, making a gruesome spotlight.

Navarre sprawled on the floor, motionless. Blood coated his shirt, his hands, and pooled on the floor beneath him.

Just outside the light, Captain Savard knelt beside his lord, head hanging, chin to chest, his breathing harsh and uneven.

"Is he..." Soren began, but stopped himself from saying the word. The thought alone was horrifying.

"No. I fed him, but I didn't have enough. I could only close the wound. He's not conscious and won't take more. I've tried." Captain Savard struggled to catch his breath. Young features twisted in pain, he pressed his hand against his side, where his own blood continued to spill from that deep gash. "Take Navarre below and hide him. Do you hear me? Hide him. Come back for Steffen. He needs your vein."

Captain Savard fought to stand, bracing himself on a nearby chair. His body nearly buckled under his own weight. He'd been weakened. Drained.

"Where's Steffen?"

The captain pointed to a shadowed corner. There, a pair of legs lay on the floor at an odd angle in the dim light, the rest hidden from sight.

The captain grunted as he pushed away from the chair, sucking in deep, readying breaths.

"Where are you going?" Soren demanded.

"To get those children."

By the time Soren had opened his mouth, Captain Savard had gone out the door and into the night.

Soren knelt at Navarre's side. Raising his head and shoulders carefully, he lifted his lord. Navarre's warm blood quickly soaked through his shirt and his hold became slippery.

"I will return, Steffen," Soren said to the dark corner.

"Forget me," Steffen replied, his breath rattling in his chest. "Only Navarre is important."

"It's nearly dawn, my friend. I won't leave you here for the sunlight. I'll be back for you. That's a promise."

His options had been seriously limited. He couldn't venture into the city carrying Navarre, so he'd backtracked to the outer corridor and slipped inside a small closet. Gently, he laid Navarre down and positioned several boxes to conceal him.

Hiding Navarre and retrieving Steffen blurred together. Steffen had been unconscious by the time he'd returned and would live, but without the immediate aid of blood, his body would take a long time to heal.

As he laid Steffen on a small cot in the clinic, a familiar tickling skittered across the back of his neck. The sun was rising. He prayed Captain Savard had found the children before the dawn claimed them. He could no longer help the captain, or the children.

———

The doors to the arena burst open, and Faith jumped, along with hundreds of other women. Almost an hour had passed since the last demon had dropped in, and the grating sound of the doors opening released a whole new batch of adrenaline racing through her.

Sword raised, she strained to see over or between the men. Not one demon had made it past the Guardians, but being unprepared wouldn't help anyone.

She waited. No swords clashing or men grunting. No fighting. The men started speaking at once, breaking the tense silence.

"Is it over?"

"Have they gone?"

Voices she didn't recognize belonging to men she couldn't see. Frustrating.

"Soren, is it safe?"

"I don't know yet," Soren answered. "I need you to keep everyone here. We're going to sweep the city before anyone leaves the safety of the arena."

Faith dropped her sword and pushed through the men. She ducked under one man's elbow, and through eyes blurred with tears, finally caught sight of Soren. He was covered in blood. Black blood, mixed with red. It coated his hands, streaked across his face, and soaked his shirtsleeve and torso. Some patches had dried, though others looked very fresh. A sob escaped her throat, and he found her instantly.

Numbing shock planted her feet in the sand, but she didn't need to move. In two long strides, he was there, his hands on her face, brushing her tears away.

"It's not all mine, Faith. I'm not hurt badly. Promise."

She nodded, hiccuping through tears, not knowing how to tell him. "Gustav...he saved me...he's..." Then she broke down, sobbing, leaning on him for strength.

"I know, Faith. I know."

Chapter 17

———

BALINESE

An impatient knock thumped a second time, and Soren threw the door open, his gun leveled at the man's head.

Captain Savard sent him a scolding look.

Soren shrugged, unapologetic. "After what happened, I wouldn't be surprised if my enemies knocked first."

"I almost wish they would," the captain said flatly.

"Everything is fine," Soren called out into his home. Elin stepped out from behind the door, a gun in her hand.

"Reinforcements?" Captain Savard asked.

"Something like that," Soren answered.

"I assume you two need to have a talk." Elin left them and joined Faith, who peeked from the bedroom.

"I'll be right back," Soren said to Faith, and she nodded. He had no desire to let her out of his sight this soon after the attack, but didn't have a choice. Thank God for Elin. She'd promised to stick close to Faith. Her presence in his home preserved his sanity, made it easier for him to step outside his door.

"I need to know where he is. He's not safe," the captain whispered. He looked utterly drawn. If he could, he'd probably be leaning against the wall for support, but constantly scanned their surroundings instead. "I heard Elin sliced through a few demons on her way to the arena."

203

"Undoubtedly. I've been training her in secret for years," Soren admitted. "If only she could be a Guardian."

The captain shot him a level look. "She's already being shunned."

"Elin knew the consequences of being trained," Soren said simply.

Soren showed the captain to a storage closet, piled high with boxes. Together they moved Navarre, careful to avoid being seen. It hadn't been a problem. Few frightened citizens had ventured from their homes. The stagnant air and dust-covered boxes proved the newly selected hiding place hadn't been touched in roughly a decade. This room, though functional, wasn't ideal. They would have to move him again.

"You're not planning on moving him again tonight, are you?" Soren asked.

"No, it's too soon," Captain Savard said, seeming to have a hard time looking away from Navarre's motionless body.

"Will he live?"

"I think the demon pierced his heart. His muscles and skin haven't healed yet. If his body can't repair the damage on its own, we'll lose him."

"Navarre has no heirs," Soren said with a sudden realization. Without leadership, the city would fall regardless of Navarre's survival. "Who is acting lord?"

"I am."

The information didn't come as a surprise. Captain Savard had greatness in him. Navarre trusted him to no end, as did Soren. He'd always been willing to follow the Captain of the Guardians to battle and death. Nothing had actually changed. The man and his principles remained the same. "What do we do now...my lord?"

"I don't know, and don't call me your lord." Captain Savard pinned him with a hard glare. "As long as Navarre lives, he is lord over this city and those who reside within. I'm only keeping his people safe until he awakens."

Captain Savard strode to the door and opened it, waited for him, and when he'd walked through, locked it behind them.

"Do you intend to take on both duties of lord and captain?" Soren asked.

"No. I need an acting captain. Can I count on you?"

"Always." He bowed his head slightly in respect.

"The council meets in twenty minutes," Captain Savard said.

"Right. What's left of it," Soren bit out.

"A new council must be created. You will join, as will Ivan."

"Ivan? Are you sure?" Ivan had been an impressive Guardian long ago, but his volatile temper left much to be desired.

"He's dedicated to the survival of the vampire race. That's all I care about." The look the captain gave him demanded he drop the conversation.

Ivan, young and lean, eased himself into the plush council chair with all the grace of a predator. His blue jeans and white T-shirt fit perfectly with his short-cropped hair.

"Someone want to tell me why these things didn't drool and sport their usual sallow look?" Ivan asked, his tone as casual as his appearance.

Soren glanced at Captain Savard. "At least he's observant."

Ivan glared, but ignored him and turned to the captain. "So what are they?"

Captain Savard stood at the head of the table. Even in his new position, he looked like he had no desire to sit through a meeting. "We don't know."

Ivan lifted his cup, took a lazy sip of coffee. "Great, let's just announce that to the public."

"Their eyes were red," Captain Savard said. "They were demons, or some variation thereof."

"Not all of them had red eyes, my lord," Ivan returned.

That newly divulged information threw the room into dead silence.

Soren's heart sunk as he stared across the table at Ivan. Had he truly said the unthinkable?

"Are you saying vampires attacked us?" the captain asked, his voice hushed.

"Not exactly." Ivan leaned forward over the table. "Two walked along like one of our kind, then attacked Sampson. I pulled one off him and fought the blue-eyed devil. I thought he was vampire, until his eyes turned red."

"Its eyes changed colors?" Soren asked.

"They did," Ivan said.

"Without yellowish skin and constant red eyes, they look like you and me," the captain mused. "Any one of us could be demon and we'd never know."

That new concern could have horrible consequences. "How long did they live down here with us, as one of us, until the attack? Are some still here?"

"There's no way to know for certain. No instances in my reports stood out in this capacity." Captain Savard shook his head slowly. "From this moment on, no one enters Balinese, and no one leaves. Not yet."

The city was on lock down, which he'd only witnessed once before on the night Navarre's father had been assassinated. Wait...had Navarre been alone when the attack began? "Ivan, you said Sampson was with you."

Ivan nodded. "I sounded the alarm, and Sampson went straight for Navarre."

"Sampson died protecting Navarre," Soren said.

"I know." Ivan's voice was tight, guarded. "They even got the good doctor in his home."

"Elin's father." Soren shook his head. How was he going to tell her?

Ivan pushed the empty cup away from him. "Bareth died."

"What?" Fists clenched on tabletop, Captain Savard leaned toward Ivan. "When? Why wasn't I told?"

"I let him know his boy was safe, like you asked me to, Captain. I followed him home so he could check on Gretta. She was dead. Killed by the demon who took their boy." Ivan raised sorrow-filled yes, shaking his head. "He went straight into the sun. I couldn't stop him."

Head hung, Captain Savard took a deep breath, then quietly said, "Bareth is a great loss."

"So many dead. Sampson. Flynn died with Nero. Their wives died struggling to keep their children safe. Julian and Yasmin..." Soren couldn't say it, and raised a shaking hand, covering his mouth. He didn't have to say a word. Everyone here knew demons had torn Julian and Yasmin apart and taken their children, left them to bleed out on the floor of the dining hall.

"Whoever choreographed this attack wanted Balinese," Captain Savard said with certainty.

"Why would any demon want a vampire city?" The notion baffled Soren.

"Precisely. They wouldn't. Not for any reason I can come up with," Captain Savard said, then fixed his gaze on him. "Soren, train and accept every man requesting to take on the responsibilities of a Guardian. If none request, knock on doors. I want our numbers doubled in a week, tripled in two."

"Tripled?" Did his captain have any idea of the staggering effort it would take to accomplish this task? "It's impossible."

"Under the old ways, it would be impossible. Every Guardian we have at this moment is now a trainer. The people of this city are doomed if they can't defend themselves. You know this, Soren. You saw how the men cowered in the arena with the women while our Guardians died. We cannot protect those we love by will alone. Teach them. This *won't* happen again."

"You think they'll try again so soon?" Soren asked him, easing forward in his chair.

"Whatever they wanted, they didn't get. I pray to God I never see their likes again, but I will not be unprepared."

"We don't know what they were after," Ivan said. "We think they failed, but how do we know they didn't succeed?"

"What do you mean?" Captain Savard asked, Ivan now his sole focus.

"Technically, the head of the snake has been cut off," Ivan supplied. "Navarre may not be dead, but he's certainly not lord at the moment. Maybe that's all they wanted."

Soren sighed heavily, scrubbing his hand across his face. "Except they pursued Captain Savard just as doggedly, almost like they knew he was the heir."

The captain paced in a tight circle. "They attacked Sampson, Navarre's personal guard, as if they knew where he would be. They targeted the lord, his heir, the High Justice, and the council. They killed the only doctor skilled enough to save a life in peril. They even targeted you, Soren, our most valued trainer. These demons knew what they were doing. This was plotted and planned meticulously. Balinese was meant to fall."

Disgust made bitterness scratch Soren's throat. Hatred burned. "We had been attacked from the inside long before Steffen called in the breach at the gates. He was stabbed from behind, then they sliced through his hamstrings."

Ivan drew in a sharp breath, thoroughly appalled.

Jaw clenched, anger seething from him, the captain said, "It was a trap. The whole thing was a trap. The demon executed in the arena was their signal. They used the children to lure Navarre away from our protection. Flynn's daughter, Nero's daughter, Sampson's daughter,

Bareth's son, and both of Julian's children had been taken. They stole children Navarre knew. Children he cared for. Then stabbed him through the heart after he'd charged above to save them."

"The children?" Since the moment he'd seen Captain Savard return alive, he'd been afraid to ask.

Captain Savard bowed his head. "We only lost one. The rest, though without their parents, are perfectly fine."

"With so many demons and the sun rising, how did they survive?" Ivan asked.

"You wouldn't believe me if I told you." The captain shook his head, unfolded a piece of paper and handed it to Soren, efficiently changing the subject. "Now. We have another problem."

Soren read the short note then passed it to Ivan.

"Thank God he wasn't here when they attacked. Vidor has family?" Soren asked his captain.

"Apparently." Captain Savard looked less than pleased.

"He even sounds stuffy when he writes," Ivan said with a cringe, then read the letter aloud. "*My niece, whom I love dearly, must be protected at all costs. I am leaving my home to warn the council of Galbraith out of concern for her safety. My apologies.*"

Though Soren didn't much care for the man, genuine relief filled him. "The road to Galbraith is long. It may be days before he returns, but at least he's alive."

"As Galbraith is now warned, we have no choice but to warn the rest. It would be diplomatic suicide otherwise. And we now have a solid reason to alarm them." Captain Savard rubbed his smooth chin, then as if he'd suddenly came to a decision, nodded sharply. "Soren, prep Titus and Dyre. Have them warn Talvane."

Soren shook his head. The loss of two Guardians seemed excessive. "You're sending two men into Paris?"

"Demons are lurking in Paris," the captain replied. "If one dies, the other had better return alive. I want to know what the hell's going on out there."

"What of Valenna?" Ivan asked.

"Send someone," the captain said dismissively.

"I'll go." The words flew from Soren's mouth, and it took him a second to register what he'd volunteered to do.

"No, you will not," Captain Savard said swiftly, the muscles in his jaw tense. "Send someone else."

"There is no one else. What Guardians we have left need to be here, patrolling the city. You can't go. Who's left? Ivan? How well do you think that would go over? He's not exactly the kind of person a royal would speak with." He sent an apologetic look to Ivan. "I mean no offense."

"None taken," Ivan said with a slight shrug. "And I don't want to go."

"Fine. We warn the other cities first. We can raise Balinese off her knees tomorrow." Captain Savard ended the meeting in the most unusual way. He simply walked out the door.

Soren stared after him. The metric ton of information dropped on them in this meeting shell-shocked him.

"What made you offer to march into hell?" Ivan asked, wide-eyed as he searched his gaze for an answer.

"If I can save the lives of my kind, I will." His former Guardian had left behind his core principles. It defied belief. "How long has it been since you've served with Guardians? Have you forgotten our purpose is to preserve life?"

"You go to Valenna." Ivan stood, his chair squealing against the hard wood floor as it slid away from the table. Soren assumed he would leave, but he planted his palms on the table. "The only life in need of preservation will be your own."

Chapter 18

———

BALINESE

Nearly an hour ago, Faith watched with tears in her eyes as two men carelessly tossed Gustav's body into a coffin, slammed the lid shut, then carried him off. She'd screamed at them, calling them heartless, along with a few other choice names. Soren had been forced to haul her home. Now she paced their bedroom, her toes twisted into the carpet each time she turned sharply.

"Why would they treat him like garbage off the street?" she raved, scrubbing another tear from her cheek.

"When a vampire passes from this world, a prayer is said for their soul, and the body is left for the sun to burn. The ash that was once our body will feed the sacred earth we live within." Reciting the words to explain the death of a vampire as if he read from a textbook helped keep his emotions in check. "Demons and murderers are dealt with differently. They are completely sealed in coffins, which prevents their decomposing bodies from seeping out into the nurturing soil and spreading evil to the good things growing in the earth. Stalkers are seen as murderers."

"It's not right. Gustav was a good man."

"This is not a perfect world, Faith, and customs are not easily broken." He pulled her down beside him on the edge of their bed.

"I'm tired and numb." She leaned into the shelter of his solid frame. "Our city will never be the same again."

Soren smiled, a small, secret smile. She had claimed Balinese as her city. Mourned the loss of its people. She was one of them.

He closed his eyes, taking a deep breath. "The demons who attacked you above, and us down here, were nothing like those of old."

"What do you mean?"

"Demons are vicious, mindless creatures. They kill for the joy of killing. The ones I remember had a yellowish-colored skin that seemed to sag and hang from their bones. Their mouth would constantly salivate from the thought of its next meal. And their eyes...those eerie red orbs flared when they looked at their prey. No one could mistake a demon for anything other than what it was." Soren stared straight ahead, seeing into the past. He'd fought them many times in his young and reckless days. They'd been easy to recognize and thus, kill. These demons, with their blue eyes and vampire looks... How could they spot those deceptive creatures among their own people?

Faith shivered at his description. "If that's a demon, then what did I see?"

"An entirely different creature. We don't know what they are." He paused a moment to let the horrifying thought pass, then said, "We have no idea what they're capable of."

"But they can be killed. I saw them die."

"They can, but these things look just like us. One of them changed the color of its eyes. What if they all can? We have to protect Balinese, and all other vampire cities. They need to know that those who live among them could be demons." And now for the words he had avoided since he'd returned. "Tomorrow I leave to warn a city not far from us."

"What? Let them send someone else," she begged, gripping his arms tightly.

He brushed a stray lock of hair from her face, stroking her cheek gently as he tucked it behind her ear, letting her hair slip through his fingers. "Faith, listen to me. If I don't go, thousands of vampires could die. Demons prefer the weaker, easier targets, like women and children. I can't stand by and let that happen. We have to warn them. I must go."

"Don't go." She looked up at him, her eyes shimmering with unshed tears.

"When I leave, Elin will stay here with you. I don't want you alone, not after..." He closed his eyes, unwilling to speak the words floating around in his head.

Another tear slipped down her cheek, but she ignored the falling drop. She took his face in her hands. "Tonight I've seen how fleeting life can be, even for your kind. Right now I have you in my hands, and I'm going to make this time count."

The sun had set. Time to go. He carefully moved her arm from across his chest. Whatever else happened, they'd had this time together. He'd loved her until she'd trembled in his arms. He'd waited his whole life for her, and she'd been perfect.

He trusted Ivan's warning about Valenna. Ivan had heard many rumors of death, disorder, and demons inside the nearby city. An ordinary vampire would not have a chance to hear this information. The news, though sinister, would be helpful. Now he'd be aware of the possibility he might be walking into the city and announcing a demon threat to a demon.

Even more worrisome, Valenna had remained eerily quiet over the last ten years. His experience increased his chance of survival greatly, but the odds were not in his favor.

If he died, Faith would be alone, and would be given to another for safekeeping.

"Not going to happen," he said through clenched teeth, leaned over and brushed back her hair, and smoothly sank his teeth in. She let out a dreamy sigh and slid her fingers through his hair, held him to her neck.

"Soren," she moaned, then her strength left her and her eyelids slowly shut. He'd taken enough to send her into a blissful unconsciousness for a short time. It was necessary. If she woke, he wouldn't have the strength to leave her.

"Remember me," he whispered, leaving his bite open and unhealed.

Faith opened her eyes to a quiet, empty room. She wanted to hold Soren one more time before he left, but the absence of his solid weight beside her crushed her hopes.

He was gone.

The breakfast tray several feet from the bed drew her attention. She had to move. If she stayed in bed any longer she would cry, so she wrapped the sheet around herself and plodded sleepily over to the table.

The tray had been filled with her favorite pastries and fruit, accompanied by a glass of red wine. She smiled and shook her head. A vampire's love of wine for any occasion continued to baffle her.

A small place card had been propped in front of the wine. She lifted the card. In bold red letters, it simply said *I love you*. Tears streamed down her cheeks, but her smile grew wider. She raised the glass, holding it up to the note in mock toast.

"And I love you," she said, then downed the entire glassful.

The sweet wine warmed her belly. Flopping back on the bed, she stared at the ceiling, still smiling. He loved her. She'd seen it in his eyes, but this giant red banner was a resounding proclamation.

A dull ache rolled in her stomach. Eyes squeezed shut, she fought through the nausea, and sat up. She should have eaten something. Alcohol before breakfast was not a brilliant idea.

As she reached for food, her body shivered violently, forcing her to stop. Chills raced over her, though her skin had become scorching hot.

Still wrapped in the sheet, she tucked herself under the thick comforter, attempting to even her temperature. She hadn't been this sick in years. Maybe she should call Elin.

After a few minutes, her teeth stopped chattering and she rubbed her temples. The building headache came as no surprise, but she fought it the moment her eyes watered and her nose tickled like she would sneeze. She didn't, and the odd sensation grew, until it became uncomfortable. Her upper teeth ached.

"Ouch," she said as she pierced her bottom lip with... Oh, no.

She jumped from the bed and ran, gripping the sheets with one hand, reaching for the bathroom door with the other. She swayed before the mirror. If her jaw hadn't already been open, looking for what she suspected might be there, it would have dropped.

Fangs. They weren't large or ferocious, but small, dainty. Feminine. Short enough to easily hide, long enough to accomplish their intended task. She looked like an idiot, puckering her lips and pulling them back as she adjusted to the bizarre feel of the two slightly longer teeth.

"You have fangs," Elin said flatly from where she hovered in the doorway.

Faith jumped. Where had she come from? "I know. It happened just now."

Elin shook her head, sharply, and certain. "Fangs don't just happen, Faith. You drank his blood."

Faith wrinkled her nose in disgust. "Yuck. I did not. I think he must have bitten me too many times."

"Impossible. He could drink from you every day until your veins ran dry and you'd still be human," the small woman said, then chewed her bottom lip as she pondered this puzzle. "Did you drink anything this morning? Last night?"

"Only the wine." She pointed to the table.

Elin lifted the wine glass, gave it a thorough investigation, then snagged the place card from the tray.

"Hey, that's private," Faith protested, marching to her.

"It most certainly is," Elin said, and flipped the card over as she handed it back.

The words on the other side of the card said *forgive me*. "I don't understand. Forgive him for what?"

"He turned you. He put his blood in the wine, and you drank it. You're vampire." Elin froze the moment the words had left her mouth. "You said he bit you. Did he bite you last night?"

"Yes, or this morning. Maybe both," she admitted, her cheeks heating.

"Where?"

Lifting her hair, she exposed her neck.

Elin sucked in a deep breath, then nodded toward the mirror. "Go have a look."

She'd expected bloodied puncture wounds, or some other such horror. Nope. Not even close. Two symmetrical and delicate black lines swirled along the right side of her neck, originating from his bite. They created a beautifully distinct design.

"You've been mated." If Elin had attempted to hide the amusement in her voice, then she'd failed miserably.

"Mated?"

"He married you, but more permanently."

"He married me without telling me?" Her girlish fantasies of planning her dream wedding had just been completely trampled. "Why would he do that?"

Elin shook her head, her long, wavy hair shifting over her slender shoulders. "I don't know. It doesn't sound like something Soren would do."

"He could have married me without turning me vampire," she grumbled, shifting her lips around her fangs.

Elin straightened suddenly. "You're right, Faith. He could have."

"I thought so." She sat on the bed, tucked the sheet under her legs. "It'll be nice to have you on my side when he gets back."

"No. You don't understand. He could have married you without marking you or turning you. But he did both without your knowledge." Her eyes widened. "You didn't have a chance to object."

"Right. I think we've established this already."

Elin let out a tired sigh. "Those fangs and that mark on your neck clinched your position as a vampire and Soren's wife. You're a free woman with the right to his wealth and status. Don't you see what he did?"

"I realize these are good things, but it should have been my decision."

Elin shook her head. "You're not understanding. Being human, if something happened to Soren, you would be passed on to the next vampire male willing to buy you. You're perpetual property. What Soren did prevented that from ever happening. You're a high-ranking female now, and you'll always be safe here, even without him. Faith, he doesn't think he'll live."

"What?" She shot off the bed. "What do you mean? Why wouldn't he live?"

"I have to find out why. Stay here," Elin said, then ran out the door, leaving Faith in an uproar of emotions.

Soren hadn't said a single word about heading into danger. He'd given her the impression that his short journey down the road would be a friendly visit with the neighbors.

If he'd tricked her to secure her future and safety, whatever waited for him out there must be perilous.

Hours passed. She had dressed, and now paced constantly. Elin hadn't returned. More waiting. She had no facts to weigh, and the normally laid back Elin had run off in a panic with the assumption that Soren would die.

Elin finally burst through the door, and Faith rushed across the room to her. "What did you find?"

"Valenna," Elin growled. "The attack must have been worse than I thought. The council sent emissaries to warn other cities. Soren went to Valenna."

"What's wrong with Valenna?" Faith clasped her hands together, tucked them tight under her chin.

Elin snorted in disgust. "Valenna is a little piece of hell that found its way to the surface. It's nothing but violence and corruption."

"Why would they send him there?"

"I doubt they know," Elin said in a quieter tone. "Stalkers don't often relay the information they find to the cities. They're only concerned with us if we walk above, in their territory."

"You know a Stalker," Faith said, certain she'd found the truth. "Gustav?"

"Not Gustav, but this Stalker lives in Paris. Sometimes he roams the countryside. A few years ago he told me about Valenna, and how their lord mysteriously died. When his mate didn't walk into the sun, but instead took over his city, the people whispered murder. It couldn't be proved, and any who tried had been killed through the laws she'd corrupted. The Stalkers say she happily watches the city sink into debauchery, and allows her pitiless captain run the city as he sees fit. Some say the captain helped her kill her husband, and she has no control over her city."

"Soren has no idea what he's up against. What happens if he's denied an audience?" She dreaded the answer.

"They could turn him away, but I doubt that would happen. It's more likely he'll be jailed until they can verify who he is and what city he came from, but I can't see them making any real effort to send one of their men to Balinese for proof. Soren could be jailed for weeks." Elin paced now, tugging at her hair, deep in thought.

Faith tipped her chin up and squared her shoulders. No decision in her life had ever been this easy. "I'm going. Where's Valenna?"

"What?" Elin whipped her head around, glared at her. "Are you crazy?"

"Tell me." She didn't have time to plead and beg. His life was in danger. "If I don't get answers from you, I'll find them somewhere else. I'm going, and you can't stop me."

Elin cringed, defeated. "There's a small abbey north of us."

Chapter 19

VALENNA

Elin had instructed her to head north, and she had, frequently glancing at the compass gripped in her palm. Keeping up a brisk pace over the countryside, she moved as silently as she could in the beaded emerald gown. She'd had little choice when it came to her attire. Those in Valenna wouldn't believe her to be vampire if she strolled up to the city in jeans. She lifted the gown away from her feet, cursing it almost as much as she cursed its matching pair of heels she now held.

Each step brought her closer to an uncertain fate, and she bolstered her courage with the fact that she was now vampire. Only demons and other vampires could harm her. Oh, and the sun. She'd almost forgotten it could fry her on the spot.

On second thought, she took it back. She was officially worse off than when she'd been human.

Faith shook her head to clear the fears and doubts from her mind. They wouldn't help her find Soren.

Her bare feet sank into the cool, lush grass as she climbed the hill. A steeple stood out against the night sky just over the hilltop. This must be the abbey.

Overgrown and unkempt vines crawled from the grass and over the few steps to the door. She would have guessed it deserted if Elin hadn't told her that Valenna lay beneath the abbey, just as Balinese hid under a chateau.

She put her shoes on, took a deep breath, then let her gown drop to the ground. What she'd planed terrified her. Soren's life might depend on her pulling off a feat she'd never attempted. Acting.

Gaze fixed on the arched wooden door, she slowed and moved with languid grace. The gown swept past her ankles with each step, the beads rustled softly. With her bare shoulders catching the moonlight and the chiffon flowing around her, she no doubt looked more like an apparition than a flesh and blood woman.

Her stomach twisted in knots as she sailed into danger. Yet somehow she was able to concentrate on keeping her heels from sinking into the grass and dirt. Several minutes passed in a blink, and the abbey loomed before her.

She didn't waver from her path, not even as a tall, bulky man stepped from the shadows, blocking the entrance.

"Hello," she said in the sultriest timbre she could manage, smiling sweetly.

A second man stepped into the moonlight, leering at her through a tangled beard. Revolting. It took all the willpower she possessed to keep her lip from curling.

"I require entry to Valenna," she said regally, meeting his eyes.

The bearded man reached out, twisted his arm around her waist and crushed her against him. A broad grin broke across his face. "You want in, sweets? You have to pay me a toll first."

The other man laughed.

"I'm here to see your captain, and I doubt he would appreciate you touching something that belongs to him," she said smoothly, forcing her body to relax.

"So you want to see my captain?" His skeptical gaze swept over her. "Do you even know his name, little pigeon?"

Faith smiled, attempting sensual feminine pride. "If I told you what I call him, he'd have both our heads."

He instantly dropped his arm from her waist. She'd either become scorching hot to the touch, or he seriously feared his captain's wrath.

"Follow me," the taller man snapped, taking control of the situation. Elin had been correct. Neither man had been willing to cross their captain.

The man entered the abbey, and impatiently waited for her on the other side of the dark doorway. Faith chased after him, and kept her mouth shut. Without knowing what might give her away, she refused to take the risk.

This rescue had been based on a lot of assumptions. First, she should be placed in the captain's office. Second, the captain's office should be near the prisons. Third, the captain should be working and away from his office at this time of night. Fourth, Soren would logically be placed in the prisons. And finally, she assumed and prayed that he still lived.

How many times she'd prayed tonight, she couldn't even begin to count.

She hurried behind the man as they passed through the center of the abbey, between the simple wooden pew, and to the alter. He then turned left sharply, opened a narrow door and beckoned her inside.

Soren was in their city. She squared her shoulders and nodded, stayed on the Guardian's heels. The torches brightly lit the spiral stone staircase, creating a sense of claustrophobia.

He moved fast, and she kept pace, skimming her hand along the wall to steady her balance. The stairs ended, and she was in a rough stone corridor, much like the entry to Balinese.

The man held open the door to a small room, and waited for her to step inside. She entered, and the guard followed her in, closed the door solidly behind him. Only a desk and a single ladder-back chair stood in the room. This was not the captain's office.

The man pulled out his radio, lifted it to his lips. "I have a woman in the holding room. Says she's here to see you."

Her heartbeat skyrocketed as the captain responded immediately, "On my way."

"Now, why would a mated woman risk death to dally with our captain?" Her escort sat on the corner of the desk, making a show of scratching the underside of his chin. "Who are you?"

Faith had no answer. She'd already used her lie, and the truth wouldn't help her.

A pounding knock on the door saved her, for the moment. The man jumped off the desk and gripped the handle, swung open the door.

An arm shot into view and punched the man right in the nose. He stumbled backward, dazed, shaking his head, his vision probably unclear. Then he was struck again. Harder. This time he crumpled, his head thumping against the stones as he landed.

Elin popped in, dressed head to toe in black, her hair slicked away from her face in a ponytail. "Are you all right?"

"You knocked him out. How did you do that?" The man had towered over Elin.

"Brass knuckles on a knife hilt. Don't leave home without it," she said, showing the weapon. "Better than breaking my fingers on his ugly face."

Elin stepped over the man and grabbed his arm. Faith took the other. Together they towed his heavy body fully into the room.

"I think you broke his nose," Faith said, eyeing him as if he would wake at any moment.

"He'll live. Let's go." Elin dashed for the door.

Faith grabbed her arm, pulled her to a stop. "He radioed the captain. He's on his way here."

"Then let's go fast." Elin peeked out of the room, then motioned for her to follow.

In the movies, heroines running in heels got caught by the bad guys, so she took them off and dropped them, stepped over the unconscious man and raced after Elin. The ran straight ahead, into what hopefully, would be the heart of the city.

It didn't take long before the corridor branched into an odd four-way intersection. The left and right had been straight and clear, but they needed to go forward. The corridor straight ahead arched to the left. Danger would be impossible to see coming, but Elin surged ahead, and she ran after her.

The chatter of approaching men echoed from ahead of them. Elin's outstretched arm smacked her in the stomach, stopping her from going any farther. Elin, like a statue beside her, stood still for a moment, listening.

"Durant isn't answering," a volatile male shouted. "Get to the holding room. Now."

Heavy footsteps followed those words. Heart pounding furiously, she and Elin spun around, and sprinted back the way they'd come. She couldn't keep pace.

At the vacant intersection, Elin grabbed her arm, pulling her to the left. After shooting past a closed door on the right, two tall doors on the left, finally there was hope. Music seeped down the hall through a door cracked open ahead.

Having been tugged inside by her companion, when faced with a crowd of people scattered throughout the room, she wanted to turn around and run again.

Elin squeezed her shoulder, not allowing her to retreat. "The best place to hide is in a crowd. You can do this."

She and her friend drew a curious glance or two, but to Faith's utter dismay, they were not questioned or stopped. In this bar-like atmosphere, everyone simply went back to the rather unsavory things they'd been doing.

A decent sized man stalked to them, and she nearly bolted, but Elin still gripped her shoulder. The man snatched a drunken beauty several feet from them, and tossed her over his shoulder. He carried her to the bar and pressed her against the counter as he drank from her neck in the middle of a full room of people.

"I thought that was..." Faith didn't finish the sentence, or look away.

"It's as private and personal as sex. At least it should be." Elin kept moving, slipping through the crowd.

Elin pulled her out of the way, preventing her from being crushed by two rowdy men. They pulverized each other with their fists and their friends tossed coins onto the table, betting on the winner.

"It's an underground Tortuga," Faith said in horror.

"And then some. A pirate wouldn't last long here." She pointed out the man who had started using his teeth to win the fight. Faith didn't have a chance to voice her disgust. Elin grasped her hand and tugged, shifting her attention. "There's another door."

Careful to avoid eye contact or bump into anyone on the way out, they weaved through the room. They didn't have time to start a fight, let alone finish one. Elin peeked out the door, then swiftly ducked back inside.

"Now," Elin said, and darted from the room, heading for the same corridor the Guardians had just run through.

"Are you sure?"

"They're headed for the entrance. If that Guardian wakes up he'll describe us perfectly. We don't have much time." Elin whipped around the corner.

At her friend's heels, Faith whispered between gulps of air, "Where's the prison?"

"We need to find the arena. Every city has one, and the prisons are always below. It should be in the center of the city."

"How do we know where the center is?"

"Good question. Should be near the gardens." Elin paused where a Y-junction split the corridor. Two identical corridors lay before them, their carved wooden arches seeming tacked on as an afterthought. These hallways had no rhyme or reason. The rounded walls and low ceilings gave the impression that these people had tunneled through without intending to stay.

"They look the same," Faith said, her shoulders slumped. They couldn't separate, and if their guess was wrong it could cost them dearly.

"Stay here." Elin ran several feet up the left corridor, stopped, stood completely motionless, then returned and darted down the corridor to the right.

Faith glanced behind them, flinching at every rolling echo.

"Left," Elin said suddenly, and in a heartbeat they took off.

"Why left?" Her bare feet slapped the cool stones as she raced to keep up with Elin.

"The left side was warmer. A garden would need the heat," Elin said as she ran, repeatedly looking over her shoulder.

The dim corridor brightened as it curved left gently, and Faith stepped into the humid garden air. The tunnel walls opened wide, and the stone floor disappeared, replaced by a mossy pathway. Trickling water bounced off the thick leaves above, dripping around them in this created jungle.

No people strolled along. No Guardians kept watch. Good for them, but strange.

Fifteen-foot trees stood to her left, too tall to see over, but to her right a massive round wall peeked through thick, green vines.

"There." She pointed, and they were running again.

Ignoring the main doors, they followed the giant wall away from the gardens and into a dark, barren corridor.

Elin stopped at a small door and pushed it open quietly, listening for movement. The stench of blood and rotted flesh swept up the stairwell. Faith's stomach lurched. They'd found the jail.

"Sounds clear. Go on down. Find Soren." Elin hustled her through the door.

"I can't leave you alone."

"That captain isn't stupid. He'll end up here. Move fast." Elin pulled her knife out, prepared to stand her ground for them.

Soren was all that mattered, and trying to change her protector's mind, a waste of precious time. The damp, chilled air engulfed her as she raced down the stairs. She paused as her feet hit the dirt floor. The open area before her was empty, the inanimate occupants two tables and a dozen chairs. No guards to stop her search.

The single light over the tables didn't illuminate the cells, and without light, she wouldn't be able to find Soren unless she peered into each cell.

She searched the grim aisle to her left first because the light shone slightly brighter there. The combination of dirt and stone grated on her feet, but it didn't slow her down.

Her vision had improved some with her change to vampire, but dark was still dark, and she strained to find a person in each cell. The prisoners hadn't been helpful. They melted into the darkest corners.

The man in the first cell was too thin and short. The second was a woman, and the third, dead.

———

Soren propped his left side against the stones. Each muscle contracting sent shards of pain skittering through his insides. Knowing what a good bleeding accomplished and experiencing one firsthand were two entirely different things. His body had weakened immediately, rendering him helpless, like he'd been drugged. The journey to this fetid prison, or what had been said around him, remained a haze. It had been easy for the Guardians to haul him into a jail cell.

He'd done his duty, stood before the lady of Valenna and her council, relayed vital news. He believed their concern genuine, until the captain bled him. All the experience in the world wouldn't have prepared him for their treachery.

Eyes closed, he let his head sag against the bars. They would come to kill him eventually. Sooner rather than later, if they were smart.

"Soren." A harsh feminine whisper reverberated through the dank prison. "Where are you? I can't see anything."

His heart dropped to his stomach. No. It couldn't be. "Faith?"

Soft footsteps rushed toward him, then he saw slender fingers grasped the bars. She knelt, peering into the cell. As she caught sight of him propped up in the corner, she smiled.

Using the bars, he hauled his drained body to her. Pain splintered through his flesh, but at least he could move. Unable to stand, he sat in the dirt and reached for her hands.

"You're hurt." She scrambled to find the injury, searching him frantically. At the sight of his ribs, she stilled.

Though now in the muted light, he didn't have to inspect himself to know fresh blood had soaked through his shirt.

"You shouldn't be here," he said, but his attempt at stern and commanding fell short. The effort sent pain like needles through his insides. "Get out."

"I won't leave, not without you." Eyes wide, the look in them expectant, she shook her head sharply.

"They'll hurt you. You need to go." He pressed a kiss on her fingers and let go of her hands.

"Damn you, Soren. You're stuck with me. I'm not going anywhere." Small form stiff, she tipped her chin up. She'd fight him on this until they locked her in with him. It was there in her eyes.

"Fine. Then how, exactly, did you plan on getting me out?"

"I don't know. The plan was to find you." The disparaging look she sent the lock broke his heart. "Maybe there's a key down here."

"No keys. The captain wears them on his belt." He sighed and lowered his head. "We can't leave unless I feed from you. I can't feed from you the way I need to. It would kill you."

"No you won't." Faith smiled, showing off her new front teeth. "Elin wouldn't let me leave until I fed."

"From who?" he demanded, jealousy ripping through him, regardless of the situation at hand.

"From Elin. And that was just weird." She wrinkled her nose.

A strangled cry came from above. Through the dim light, the lifeless body of a man thumped down a few steps. Had the captain killed one of his own?

Slim legs followed, dodging the corpse. Then Elin appeared, skipping the last three steps entirely.

"Six coming," Elin snapped.

"Go, Elin. Get out of here," he urged, but she didn't budge.

"I stay," she said, bracing her legs as she reworked her grip on the knife.

Grasping the bars with both hands, he towed his body upright, leaned heavily against the iron for support. "Elin, you're a Guardian. My Guardian. You will follow an order when it's given."

With a defiant look, Elin disappeared.

A hard-voiced, angry man bellowed from the top of the stairs, "Did you bother asking her name?"

"I only detained her," the nervous Guardian said from farther away.

"Find her, or I'll have you gutted," his superior barked.

"We're leaving," Soren whispered, drawing Faith's rapt attention from the Guardians. "Press your neck to the bars."

She didn't waver, pressing her neck between the bars tightly.

"I'm going to take a lot from you, and fast. You will pass out," he said quickly.

She nodded, and he bit her, his arm crushing her against the bars. This was not the passion-laced feeding they had shared before. This was urgent, rough. He felt her weakening, fading under his palms.

She lost consciousness, and he sealed her flesh closed and clutched her waist. He wouldn't let her drop.

As her blood surged through him, he pressed his forehead against the bars. Vampires didn't take this much blood. He needed the strength, but the drunken sensation rushing through his body sapped his energy, and he struggled to keep Faith off the ground. His vision became hazy for a moment, and then the overindulgence paid off. Warm, tight burning spread over his left side, and his wound knit together from the inside out.

Soren caught the captain's gaze over her head, sent him a deadly glare. A second later he and Faith disappeared from the cell.

––––––––––

He hadn't let Faith out of his arms since they'd returned home. The very first time her eyes had fluttered open, he'd kept her awake long enough for her to feed from him. With that feeding, he had acquired two symmetrical swirling marks to match the ones he had given her. The identical marks of Possession declared them fully mated.

She'd slept heavily for the first few hours, her body mending from the shock of losing so much blood. Warmth had finally returning to her limbs, proof she'd soon recover.

Faith woke, her breathing panicked and her hands flying out to catch hold of anything solid. "Soren?"

"We're home," he whispered. With a deep sigh, she relaxed into his embrace.

"We made it out," she said, her wispy tone filled with wonder and relief, and she skimmed her fingers over his cheek.

"We're fine." He kissed the top of her head.

"Are we? How do you know?"

"You're still here with me," he said softly.

"We're stuck together forever, then?" Faith smiled, a shy and inviting kind of smile he'd begun to love.

He kissed her smiling lips, and planned on kissing every part of her that he'd thought he might never touch again. With her in his arms, this contentment would never end. Smiling, he pressed his forehead to hers. "It's not nearly long enough."

He'd lost so much in such a short time. Guardians, friends, all destroyed by demons. But through some miracle, he'd held on to what had become most important to him.

Faith.

Epilogue

_____

BALINESE

Soren watched the woods. Did demons wait outside of his home, or yet from within? He'd walked past four Guardians posted inside the chateau, and eight patrolled the entire property above ground. The increased numbers might be enough to stave off another attack, but he had no way of knowing for certain.

Steffen leaned hard on the wall, staring out into the night. He'd walked for the first time tonight, and he'd ended up at his gate.

"Steffen, how are you?" Soren addressed the man beside him, half hidden in the shadows.

"If you're asking about my injuries, I'm fine. If you're asking about the sun, those demons gave me one hell of a reason to live," his friend said through clenched teeth, and likely a great deal of pain.

"Good." They only had a minimal number of fully trained Guardians. He needed Steffen.

"If you catch another demon, I want in the arena." Steffen's tone had slipped into something dark and hateful.

"Done," Soren agreed. "Your feet will be in the same sand, Gatekeeper. That I promise you."

After the attack, Steffen had become a different man, as had he. Fear changed people. For the first time in centuries, the people of Balinese feared the world above.

Keep reading for a special sneak peek of Jen Colly's

BOUND

Chapter 1

———

Morley twisted the hilt of the dagger into his fist as he scanned the wide hall behind him. Still empty. The eerie quiet should have helped, made him more comfortable with his stealthy approach. It didn't. The plush red carpet, dim lights, and massive framed paintings made him feel like he traipsed through a tomb. He shouldn't be here.

Inset beneath a deep arch trimmed in gold, he found the door, framed with pillars and a mock roof overhang. He approached the door, stood close enough for his nose to touch the white wood. Bolts and locks no doubt secured the door from the inside. He didn't need a key.

Drawing in several long, deep breaths, he struggled to transform, to shift into his Spirit. When the change finally washed over him, he disappeared, completely invisible. A ghost. In this form, he took a single step and easily passed through the door.

He could only manage that single small feat. On the other side of the door, he couldn't hold his Spirit, and he appeared, reaching out to the door to steady his wobbling muscles. Exhausted, Morley panted for breath. His body had never tolerated the change well.

At least he didn't have to worry about disturbing his target. She lived alone, and at this time of day, should be sound asleep. Creeping past her expensive furniture and fancy knickknacks displayed on random, useless little tables, he ventured farther into her home. The glass double doors to her bedroom were closed, and as he eased one open, he caught a glimpse of the sleeping woman. Arianne. The Lady of Galbraith.

He'd never killed anyone before, didn't know exactly how he'd do it, only that it must be done. Personally, he didn't care one way or another. The last royal left in the city, her death would end the bloodline. When gone, another stuffy aristocrat would take her place. Nothing would ever truly change for those of his lower class, but he wasn't here for a change. He was here to do a job.

Morley edged toward her bed. Fluffy pillows, more than he'd seen in his lifetime, lay piled near the top of her bed. Several smaller, purely decorative lacy pillows surrounded her. Yep, he was jealous. He'd gone without luxuries most of his life, often counting himself darn lucky to have a door to temporarily shut out the rest of the world. Soon, using the money he'd get from this job, he could finally purchase his freedom. No longer a servant, he'd walk away from this city with the shirt on his back and enough money in his pocket to buy a decent life somewhere else.

The lady lay curled on her side facing him, a downy white comforter tucked under her satin-clad arm. Vampires didn't die easily, a gift to his species from whatever god had created them, but if he drove the blade directly into her heart, she'd be dead in a few minutes. Unless, of course, she'd just fed.

Roll her onto her back. Stab her. It would be that easy. Again he twisted the dagger in his fist, readying himself to finish the deed swiftly. His knees touched the edge of the mattress. Weapon raised in the air, he reached out to move her.

A heavy body crashed into him, tackled him solidly from shoulder to hip. He landed on the floor hard, his breath momentarily squeezed from his lungs. What the hell?

Face smashed into the carpet, he couldn't see a thing. The sharp jab of a knee ground into the center of his back. Morley tried to lift his head, to take a look at the man he hadn't realized was in the room, but the man planted his forearm across the back of his neck, reunited him with the thick carpet.

Covers rustled, followed by a soft gasp. Lady Arianne was awake. A sleepy feminine voice called out into the darkness, "Are you all right?"

The man kept him pinned to the floor and didn't answer her, and all Morley could see was the carpet, his fallen dagger, and chair legs. The soft snick of a bedside lamp switch flooded the room with a mellow light, and a pair of bare feminine feet padded into sight.

"My lady," Morley said, the words a labor with the weight of the man on his back. "I meant you no harm. Please, have mercy on me."

"Mercy?" The lady reached down to retrieve his dagger from the floor. "You Spirit into my bedroom at midday with a knife in your hand, and you dare to beg me for mercy?"

He tried again, not above begging. "Please. The knife was just...I would never—"

"Enough," she snapped, and the harshness of her tone stunned him into silence. The man above him shifted, and Morley suddenly realized that the single word, sharp and final, had been meant for the brute on top of him.

Morley cried out as the burning pain of a knife sliced deep into his side, and then the blade twisted cruelly as it left his body. The gaping hole was draining a good amount of his blood, and with it, any remaining strength.

"No need to kill him," she said to the other man. "The captain is on his way."

Within seconds his body had lost the ability to fight, his muscles weak, unresponsive. His wound throbbed, and he longed to curl up where he lay. The man shoved him as he stood and backed away, leaving Morley sprawled on the floor, his blood seeping into the lady's carpet.

Morley wouldn't die from the wound, and that was the point of a bleeding. Drained and weak, his body would put every ounce of strength into repairing itself from the inside out, and unless he fed, he would remain in a debilitated state. But this man had twisted the knife as it left his body, and the act felt personal. Whoever this man was, Guardian or servant, he was vicious.

"Give me the knife," the lady commanded his attacker in a hushed voice. "Now go."

The door burst open, and the rush of multiple footsteps shook the floor beneath him. Guardians surrounded him, hauled him to his feet, secured and stabilized him.

"Excellent timing, Captain," she said.

The captain, a beastly sized man, surged toward her only to stop short when he saw the lady held a bloody knife in her hand.

"Are you hurt?" the captain asked as he took the knife from her hand. Lady Arianne faced him, her mauve satin nightdress sweeping the floor, black hair curling around her arms in loose waves.

She shook her head, proud and seemingly unaffected. "No. I am unharmed."

"My lady," Morley begged again. "Please let me speak."

Chin tipped, shoulders squared, she might as well be wearing her crown with an army at her back. The woman was fearless. "Is there anything you have to say that could make me believe you had no intention of murdering me?"

"I didn't follow through."

"The end result matters little when the intention is clear. Guardians, take him away," she ordered. "Captain, a word."

The Guardians dragged him away, across the plush carpet and out the door. It was late, and as they passed through the larger well-traveled corridors, no vampires roamed about. All was quiet.

The two men hauled him down the old stone stairway to the jail beneath the arena. He wanted to struggle, to fight. No use. His strength depleted, he could barely pull his feet beneath him for the next step. Even if he'd had the ability, one man would never triumph over two Guardians. Decades of training had made them terribly good at their job.

With a jarring halt, they paused before a cell. The end cell. Three walls of iron bars, one solid cement wall. This was the cell reserved for those with an execution date.

A hard shove to his right shoulder sent Morley toppling into the jail cell and rolling across the floor. Dirt-coated stone dug into his knees and forearms as he tried to stop the momentum. With a heavy squeal, the door shut, and the Guardian's key slid the lock home before he could scramble to his knees.

"You've got about twelve hours to live," a Guardian said, no longer concerned with him as they walked away.

The crunching of the scattered gravel grinding into the dirt followed them. The fading sound left behind a strange emptiness. He didn't bother attempting to stand. What was the point when his death crept closer minute by minute? He crawled to the only wall, collapsed with his back against the cold cement, head on his knees, and arms curled around his legs.

He should have known he'd end up here, most with his talent did. High-priced jobs were always on the table for those rare few with the ability to take their Spirit form and disappear momentarily.

Like an idiot, he'd jumped at the chance to rake in the cash. What did he have to show for his efforts? A gaping hole in his side and a death sentence.

The initial silence had gone, replaced by the misery of prison. Dripping water hit the floor somewhere to his left, feet shuffled to his right, and the occasional moan echoed off every wall. The plunk of a stone hitting the floor nearby brought his head up.

He wasn't alone. A lean man sat inside his cell. Morley glanced around frantically, certain the man hadn't been here a moment ago. The slashing angle of a shadow covered the top half of his body, but he was real. With an arm casually propped on his knee, the man seemed completely at ease in this filthy place. He tossed another stone.

"You had a job to do, and you failed," the man accused. "Lady Arianne should be dead."

"How did you know?" Morley asked, squinting his eyes in an effort to see through the darkness.

"Jefford Morley," his cellmate said, a smooth arrogance in his voice. "You'd better talk."

Who was he? This was not the same man who'd put him up to the job. Perhaps a Guardian had been planted in here in the hopes that he would tell a fellow villain what he might not reveal to the Guardians.

He scrubbed his hand over his face. "I don't know anything. How could I help her?"

"Who says I want to save her?"

Ah, now it made sense. Another assassin. Morley laughed, though the wound at his side kept his amusement brief. "You won't be doing much of anything sitting in here with me."

The man leaned to his left and into what little light the cell offered, and Morley strained to catch a glimpse of his face. No luck. His short beard and wild mass of curling chin-length hair kept him hidden.

"I'm only visiting. Friend." He drew out the last word, and recognition snapped through Morley like a whip. Morley's cellmate could only be one man.

"You're Bruis's son. Keir," he announced, his throat tightening. "Guardians hauled you away. I saw it. You killed old Bruis. Thought you were dead. Should be."

Keir sent him a level stare. "You're Legard's servant. What did he offer you?"

"No, not Legard. Please, my master had nothing to do with this," Morley sputtered. "A man cornered me down on Shar, where the Legards have their clothes laundered. I'd never seen him before, I swear. He offered me enough money to buy my freedom from Legard."

"Is that so?" Keir tossed a stone, then another. "I'd like to find this man."

"What I know is useless. Brown eyes and a square chin were all I could see beneath his hood. He could be anyone. Even if you found him, I doubt he'd make you the same deal." The instant the words left Morley's mouth, Keir laughed softly. Morley sucked in a quick breath. He'd been wrong. "You don't want a deal. You're the unholy thing killing men in their sleep."

Keir leaned forward. A sinister grin split his lips. White, fanged teeth flashed in the dark. Trapped inside a cell, weak with the loss of blood, Morley had no escape. What was in Keir's hand? Was it a...knife?

———————

Heavy footfalls of a Guardian approached, and Keir vanished. He'd easily taken his Spirit form, moving freely without being seen, even among his own kind. The only downfall of using Spirit was the chilled air it created around him. It would tip off the Guardians to his presence. Backing away from Morley, he tucked his invisible self into the far corner of the cell.

The Guardian glanced left and right as he sped through, no doubt rushing his turn to check on the prisoners. He'd just passed the cell when his steps faltered in mid-stride. He backtracked, leaned closer, and studied the man on the floor.

"Quint! Morley's dead!" He yanked the keys off his belt, fumbled through them. The cell door swung open just as Quint came racing down the narrow aisle, his freckled face flushed.

"It's the same knife. Red rose on a white hilt. It's him," the Guardian whispered, glancing over his shoulder. "But he's never killed in the dungeons."

"Or slit a throat." Quint motioned the Guardian into silence and brought a radio to his lips. "Captain? We have a situation in the jail."

The radio buzzed briefly before the captain's steady voice broke through. "Go ahead. What is it?"

"Cancel the execution. It's already happened."

"What?" the captain roared. "Who killed him?"

Quint stared down at Morley's corpse. "I don't know, but he was killed with a very familiar knife."

Ten seconds of silence suddenly gave way to the captain's controlled voice. "I'm about to enter a council meeting with an unexpected guest from Balinese. I can't leave. Handle it, Quint."

"Yes, sir." Quint clipped the radio to his hip. "Seal the jail. No one goes in or out, including Guardians. I want a full head count first, Guardians and prisoners, then a thorough search."

For nearly half an hour Keir watched the Guardians methodically check the jail from cell to cell, top to bottom. The captain's second in command possessed an altogether entertaining tenacity when thrown into action. Keir hated to walk away, but the lady waited.

In his invisible state, he sent Quint a mock salute, then turned, moving through the jail without giving his path much thought. He'd been here time and again, and he'd be back. Blocked walls, iron mazes, and wasting life. Home, sweet home.

Keir skirted along the walls, keeping the cooler air of his Spirit clear of the Guardians. Often that chill could be felt nearly two feet away from his location. Being captured was not part of his plan. Best not to take the chance.

The stairs carried him away from the prison to freely search for Morley's intended target. Galbraith was an oddly constructed city, the cylindrical structure diving deep into the ground with a dozen levels. Originally designed to separate nobility from the lower classes, it remained true to its purpose. The layout made finding Lady Arianne a simple task.

As Keir had just eliminated the need to execute Morley, the lady had no reason to make an appearance at the arena. Tonight being Monday, he scratched the chapel off his list. It wasn't mealtime, which excluded the dining hall. By process of elimination, if she wasn't in the council room, she'd be home.

Still cloaked in Spirit, Keir paused not far from the closed and guarded doors of the council room. Relentless bickering seeped through the doors. He cringed and turned away. Her home waited two floors above.

Reading Order

<u>The Cities Below</u>

In the Dark

Bound

Beneath the Night

Sheltered

The Guardian

Night Stalker

Don't miss out!

Visit the website below and you can sign up to receive emails whenever Jen Colly publishes a new book. There's no charge and no obligation.

https://books2read.com/r/B-A-ICLR-KSPIF

BOOKS 2 READ

Connecting independent readers to independent writers.

About the Author

Jen Colly is the rare case of an author who rebelled against reading assignments throughout her school years. Now she prefers reading books in a series, which has led her to writing her first paranormal romance series: *The Cities Below*. She will write about anything that catches her fancy, though truth be told, her weaknesses are pirates and vampires.She lives in Ohio with her supportive husband, two kids, and four rescued cats.

Read more at https://www.jencolly.com.

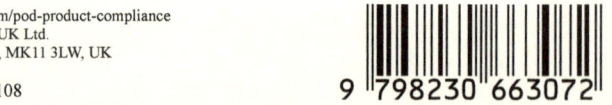